W9-CNC-566

DISCARD

CAMPBELL HILL SCHOOL LIBRARY

The Great Smith House Hustle

Other books by Jane Louise Curry

The Great Flood Mystery

The Lotus Cup

Back in the Beforetime:
Tales of the California Indians
illustrated by James Watts

Me, Myself and I

Little Little Sister
illustrated by Erik Blegvad

The Big Smith Snatch

What the Dickens!

(Margaret K. McElderry Books)

The Great Smith House Hustle

Jane Louise Curry

MARGARET K. McELDERRY BOOKS
New York

Maxwell Macmillan Canada
Toronto

Maxwell Macmillan International
New York   Oxford   Singapore   Sydney

Copyright © 1993 by Jane Louise Curry
All rights reserved. No part of this book may be reproduced or
transmitted in any form or by any means, electronic or
mechanical, including photocopying, recording, or by any
information storage and retrieval system, without permission in
writing from the Publisher.

Margaret K. McElderry Books
Macmillan Publishing Company
866 Third Avenue
New York, NY 10022

Maxwell Macmillan Canada, Inc.
1200 Eglinton Avenue East
Suite 200
Don Mills, Ontario M3C 3N1

Macmillan Publishing Company is part of the Maxwell
Communication Group of Companies.
First edition
Printed in the United States of America
2   4   6   8   10   9   7   5   3   1
The text of this book is set in Bodoni.

Library of Congress Cataloging-in-Publication Data
Curry, Jane Louise.
The great Smith house hustle / Jane Louise Curry. — 1st ed.   p.   cm.
Summary: Just after moving into their grandmother's house in
Pittsburgh, the five Smith children must uncover a long-standing
scam to steal the houses of old people before Grandma Smith loses
her home. Sequel to "The Big Smith Snatch."
ISBN 0-689-50580-9
[1. Swindlers and swindling—Fiction.   2. Brothers and sisters—
Fiction.   3. Grandmothers—Fiction.   4. Pittsburgh (Pa.)—Fiction.
5. Mystery and detective stories.]   I. Title.
PZ7.C936Gt   1993   [Fic]—dc20   92-33073

To Amy Kellman,
with thanks!

1

Sunday Evening, July 25th

ELVIRA, THE SMITH FAMILY'S OLD CHEVY VAN, COUGHED
and rattled her way off Interstate Highway 79 at the
Canonsburg exit. Belinda Rainbow—"Boo"—Smith
didn't bother to raise her head to look out. She didn't
have the energy. Even for a Sunday in July, one hundred and four degrees was *hot*. It was only a little
cooler now that the sun was down.

The Smiths had been on the road for ten days. Ten
long days. Though all of her windows were open, Elvira was a bake-oven on wheels. Boo was too miserable
and sticky hot to care that they were in Pennsylvania
at last. Pennsylvania or Peru—who cared? She was
fed up with peanut-butter-and-jelly sandwiches, fed
up with feeling grubby, and fed up with unironed
clothes even though they *were* clean. Most of all she
was fed up to the ears with her five-year-old sister,
Babba. Danny, the littlest, was no trouble. But Babba?

Babba, with her blond curls and big blue eyes, might
be cute as a basketful of kittens, but she was as fussy

as five old ladies. Worse, she was as determined as a rhinoceros at getting her own way. Worse still, she was liable to turn green and carsick if she didn't. Worst of all, she somehow always managed to feel urpish when there was no safe place for the van to pull to the side of the road. At least the supply of old plastic bags hadn't run out yet. Babba was too tidy ever to make a mess on the mattress. Except for taking turns on the passenger seat, the children rode in the rear on two old mattresses that lay on top of the cardboard boxes that held the family's belongings.

The Smiths, except for Mrs. Smith, who was still in the hospital back in Los Angeles, were near the end of their long journey. They had driven more than two thousand miles from California, headed for Grandma Smith's house in Pittsburgh, Pennsylvania. Mr. Smith had begun a new job in Pittsburgh at the Buscaglia Box Company several weeks before Mrs. Smith's illness. Because she couldn't drive Elvira and the children east, their father had to take time off and fly out to California to do so. Mrs. Smith's doctor wouldn't allow her to travel until after the new baby was born. She was to join the family at Grandma's as soon after that as she could.

Boo wished with all her heart that the whole family could have stayed in Los Angeles. Nancy Bitts and Susie Loo and every other friend she had in the world were there. Now they would all be going on to Nightingale Junior High at the end of August without her.

August. Even in August the weather in Los Angeles never got icky-sticky hot—or at least not for days and days on end. And there it always cooled off at night. Here the nights stayed icky-sticky. On the day the Smiths chugged through Memphis, Tennessee, a newspaper headline on the paper rack at Ed's Truck Stop Restaurant had read 100-PLUS HEAT WAVE FROM TEXAS TO MAINE. It had been so hot that Poppy, who was eight and thin as a Popsicle stick, had fainted dead away at the restaurant's front door. Poppy, who had been born a "blue baby" and spent a lot of time in the hospital when she was small, was still not as tall or strong as other eight-year-olds. At least that had meant the children got to sit indoors in the air-conditioning for an hour. One of the truck drivers had bought them all soft drinks and frozen-yogurt cones. Mr. Smith used some of the family's emergency fund to buy a little fan in the truck-stop shop to plug into Elvira's dashboard outlet. Everyone got to use the fan, but it was mostly for Poppy. She said she felt fine, but she looked about as fine as a damp, faded dishrag.

After Memphis, Boo in her misery had decided that if it weren't that she was going to have her own, private bedroom for the first time in her life at Grandma's, she would rather be dead than going to Pittsburgh.

It was Boo's ten-year-old brother Cisco, dozing in the front passenger seat, who sat up and rubbed his eyes as Elvira slowed. (Cisco's full name, San Francisco Moonlight Smith—even goofier than Boo's—

3

sometimes made him wish his parents were more like everyone else's.)

"Are we almost there?" Cisco peered eagerly out into the dusk, but all he could see were hills and fields and trees.

"Not yet awhile." Mr. Smith kept his voice low so as not to wake Babba and four-year-old Danny. Both were curled up fast asleep between Boo and Poppy on the mattresses in back.

"The engine's heating up again," Mr. Smith explained quietly. "Sounds like the old fan belt's pretty near had it. If we can spot a safe place to pull to the side of the road, I should be able to get it off and the spare belt on while we still have some light to see by."

Mr. Smith could, as his old boss Mr. Monahan once said, take a car engine apart and repair it blindfolded with one arm in a cast. The new fan belt was soon installed and Elvira was on her way again. Ten or twelve miles further on, in the town of Mount Lebanon, Elvira chugged into a service station and pulled up at a self-service pump.

"What's the matter now?" Boo grumbled as the door on her father's side banged shut.

"Just gas," Cisco said. "And another quart of oil."

Poppy yawned and stretched. "Poo-oo-r old Elvira the oiloholic. Where are we?"

Cisco shrugged. "I dunno. Some town."

Curiosity got the better of Boo, and she sat up to look out the window. There was little to see but streetlights, a brick building with empty shop windows across the road, and passing cars. One of two big boys riding in the back of a pickup truck that had stopped at the traffic light pointed at Elvira. Both boys stared. Boo, embarrassed, ducked down quickly. All the way across the country people had pointed or smiled at the battered old van's fat rear-end rainbow and the faded silver stars and red-and-gold planets painted higgledy-piggledy all over her dark blue sides and top. Boo didn't usually mind the van's being old. When she was little she had loved the paintings because Rainbow was her middle name and because the stars looked magical. In the last ten days, though, she had begun to feel like a grubby tiger cooped up in a ratty old circus wagon. She hated it.

As his father headed for the door to the snack shop and cashier's counter, Cisco squirmed around to hang over the back of the passenger seat.

"Did you see the traffic lights? They're a different shape from the ones at home. The streetlights are different, too. Even the gas stations. It's really int'resting. Some places look so old-fashioned, it's kind of like traveling in and out of olden times. Ever since back in Texas, all kinds of things have been getting differenter and differenter. It's almost like it's turned into another country. There's the shapes of houses, too. And so many of them are built out of bricks. Even some of the streets are made out of bricks."

"An' no place has got paper seat covers in the rest

5

room, neither." Babba sat up with a scowl. "That's not *nice*."

Boo groaned. "I thought you were asleep."

"I am," said Babba. She flopped back again.

"I like the places with brick streets," Poppy put in drowsily. "I like the way the tires go *rumbly-bumbly* on them."

A minute or two later Mr. Smith finished at the gas pump. He stuck his head in at the driver's-seat window.

"Anybody got fifteen cents? I'm fifteen cents short of ten dollars, and I don't want to break our last emergency-fund twenty-dollar bill if I don't have to."

"I've got it." Cisco dug in his pocket and counted out two nickels and five pennies.

Once the gas was paid for and Mr. Smith had added a quart of oil to the engine from their own supply, they started on their way again.

"How far's Pittsburgh?" Cisco braced himself against the dashboard as Elvira lurched over a big pothole at the service-station exit.

"Not far," his father answered. "Five, maybe six miles."

In the back, Boo stiffened. "What's that noise?"

Mr. Smith made a face. "Just another Elvira rattle. No-o-o problem."

But the rattle grew louder. A mile or so further on, Mr. Smith sighed and pulled to the side of the road again. "Where's the flashlight? Sounds like that pothole may have given the muffler a knock. If it's loose,

I'll have to wire the blamed thing up so we don't have it falling off in the middle of the Fort Pitt Tunnel."

"Tunnel?" Cisco yelped in excitement, bouncing in his seat.

"That's right. Under Mount Washington."

Poppy sat bolt upright. "Under a mountain?" she quavered.

The tunnel, once Elvira's muffler was fastened up again, proved to be as interesting as Cisco expected and as alarming as Poppy feared. Danny and Babba slept on, but Boo grew anxious. The tunnel seemed to go on and on. Its lights glared and the sounds of engines and tires echoed loudly. Poppy shut her eyes and covered her ears until Boo gave her an all-clear nudge.

"Wow-ee!" Cisco exclaimed.

Elvira had emerged onto a bridge approach. Ahead, across the river, the towers of downtown Pittsburgh sparkled in the dark like a fairy-tale city.

Fifteen minutes later the Smiths were making a right turn into Oakland Square in the part of the city known as Oakland. Two lefts around the end of the square brought them to the corner where Hillyard Street tilted downhill. Turning right, down Hillyard, the van pulled up in front of the first house below the corner.

Cisco jumped out excitedly onto Grandma Smith's front sidewalk.

Boo pushed open the rear side door of the van. "Ooh!" she exclaimed in spite of herself.

Poppy, dazzled by the bright streetlight, rubbed her

7

eyes and, with Cisco, stared in wonder at the tall old brick house. Three stories high, it had a wide front porch with a handsome stone rail and columns. A light in the front hall glowed green and gold through the front door's oval stained-glass window.

Perhaps Pittsburgh *wasn't* going to be so awful. . . .

2

Monday Morning, July 26

GRANDMA SMITH, BROKEN HIP OR NO, WAS UP BEFORE SIX o'clock the next morning making coffee, scrambling eggs, and toasting bread. Mr. Smith worked day-shift hours, repairing delivery trucks and machinery, at the Buscaglia Box Company and had to catch an early bus in order to be on the job at seven o'clock. He could not drive Elvira to work because everyone had been too tired the night before to unload her.

The children—except for Babba and Danny, who had been carried into the house sound asleep and still had not twitched—came down to their cereal and toast two hours later. They sat around the table passing the butter dish and marmalade pot and being polite. Everything felt strange. Grandma herself, whom the children had never met before, was not at all what they had expected. Her letters to California, their father's tales of growing up in Pittsburgh, his out-of-focus photographs of her—none of these had told them much. Their friends' grandmothers wore slacks and brightly colored blouses, and some were thin and colored their hair and wore dangly earrings. Not Grandma Smith. Grandma was small and plump and looked like a picture-book granny. Her dress was a faded blue with tiny white flowers all over it. Her soft, fine hair looked like a short, curly white cloud. Her house was crowded with knickknacks and mirrors and dark, old-fashioned furniture.

To add to the strangeness, the breakfast bowls and spoons, cereal box, bread and toaster, coffee pot, and milk and juice jugs and glasses were set out on a dining-room table crowded into one end of the living room. The table was in the living room because Grandma, back at the beginning of the summer when she had broken her hip, had had to have her bed moved downstairs to the dining room. She was still in a wheelchair, so the dining room was still her bedroom.

"But not for long," Grandma said. "I can push myself up now and balance on my good leg well enough to reach most of the kitchen cupboards."

Suddenly she stiffened. "Oh, drat!" She put down her coffee cup and scuttled backward in her wheelchair, away from the front window.

The children looked up from their cereal bowls in surprise. As Grandma rolled through the wide doorway into the hall, she gave a toss of her head toward the front of the house.

"Is that old woman picking my roses?" she whispered loudly. Her face wore a comically fierce expression that made Poppy giggle.

10

Three heads turned toward the wide window that looked out across the front porch and narrow patch of garden to the sidewalk and the street. There they saw a fat old woman in a black sweater, an ankle-length black dress, and pointy black shoes on tiny feet come teetering past on the sunny sidewalk. She wore her black hair pulled back into a fat bun and pushed an odd-looking cart that had a bright purple umbrella fastened to it for shade.

The old woman stopped when she came abreast of Elvira. With a scowl she tiptoed over to peer in through the van's dusty windows. Then suddenly she turned and fixed an angry glare on the house. Poppy shrank down in her chair. Even Boo felt half tempted to duck under the table.

Once the woman was safely past and gone, Cisco made a funny-scared face. "Brr! That old lady looked like she wanted to zap a curse on your house, Grandma. But she didn't pick any roses. Who is she?"

"*That* was Matilda Tuttlebee," said Grandma with a sniff.

She wheeled herself back to the table and her coffee cup. "The Wicked Witch of Hillyard Street," she explained. "She fights with everybody, but she's hated us Smiths ever since your grandpa caught her son Stanley stealing poor Mary O'Meara's eyeglasses. Grandpa gave the horrid little shrimp a good walloping, and after that the least little thing was enough to set Matilda off."

"What did she do?" asked a wide-eyed Poppy.

11

"Anything that popped into her head, I'd say. When your daddy was a toddler and his dog Toby dug up some of her daffodil bulbs, she cut down our big, old viburnum bush. Fifty years old, that bush was! Most times nowadays she doesn't bother to wait for an excuse. Last month all my roses up and disappeared. Last week it was the daylilies. I'd bet you my bottom dollar it was Tilly Tuttlebee who snipped 'em off."

"What happened to her little boy?" Cisco asked.

"Stanley? Oh, he had a fight with his father—a nasty man—and ran away when he was fourteen or fifteen. That was the last we ever heard of him." Grandma sniffed. "Too bad Tilly didn't run away, too."

Poppy tipped her bowl sideways to scoop up her last spoonful of cornflakes. "If she tries to cut off your roses, Cisco'll catch her for you, Grandma. He's practicing to be a detective."

"Is he, now?" Grandma's eyebrows lifted. "How do you practice for that, Cisco honey?"

Cisco grinned, embarrassed. "Mostly by watching TV," he admitted. "But sometimes I practice following people or collecting clues."

Grandma nodded. "Well, I'll be very pleased to know whether Mrs. Tuttlebee is the thief, but I think I'd rather not have you *catch* her. I wouldn't know what to do with her. If I report her to the police, she'll only do something nastier still, to get even."

"You could put up a fence," Boo suggested. "A tall one."

12

"We could," Grandma agreed. "But the only sort that wouldn't keep the sunshine off my roses is that ugly chain-link kind. I think I'd rather find out the truth, and then let well enough alone."

"Besides," Cisco put in, "we can't put a fence around Elvira. Mrs. Bumblebee made a face at her, too. She could let the air out of Elvira's tires easy as pie."

Grandma laughed. "Not Bumblebee. *Tuttle*bee."

Before he left for work Mr. Smith had moved the mattresses out of the back of the van and into the front hall, where they leaned against the wall. Once Babba and Danny had been wakened, dressed, and given their breakfast, the children set to work unloading Elvira.

The floor of the rear part of the van had been tightly packed with a layer of boxes and baggage. Boo and Cisco lugged the boxes holding their parents' belongings up to the front second-floor bedroom. With Poppy's help the little ones carried their own cartons of clothing, toys, and odds and ends up to the top floor. The two boys had the front bedroom overlooking the street. Poppy and Babba's room, in the middle, had two windows that looked across to the next house and down into its garden. Boo's was the small room at the back.

The house itself was an adventure. In Los Angeles most houses the children had seen were all on one floor. Some, like their own old house, were two stories tall, but only once before had they set foot in a three-story house. That one—the crooked Mr. and Mrs. Dockett's house in Los Angeles—had been *really* weird. Grandma's wasn't weird, just—different. Mr. Smith had built a ramp up one side of the porch steps for Grandma's wheelchair. And there were so many stairs! Four-year-old Danny stumped happily up and down the steep flights carrying his building blocks up two handfuls at a time until he was too tired to climb another step.

Babba's few belongings were soon tucked away in the chest of drawers she was to share with Poppy. Babba herself spent the rest of the morning exploring. For Babba that meant taking a peek into every drawer and closet and cupboard she could find. The top drawer of Grandma's dresser was best. Among the pretty, old-fashioned baubles there she found a necklace of crystal beads that sparkled like diamonds.

"Babba, you little snoop!" Boo stood in the doorway, hands on her hips. "You come out of there this minute or I'll tell Grandma."

"I didn't touch anything," Babba protested, but she pushed the drawer shut and hurried into the hall.

The next Boo saw of her, she was snuggled up with Danny in a living-room armchair next to Grandma's wheelchair. The two of them were listening wide-eyed as the old lady read them the story "The Seven White Cats."

When the story was finished, Babba sat up straight.

"That's what I want!" She fixed her grandmother with a pair of determined blue eyes. "A white kitty. You'd like a white kitty, too, wouldn't you, Grandma?"

"Who me?" Grandma Smith was startled. "To tell the truth, Babba, no. I don't believe I would."

"Oh, yes, you really will." Babba nodded her blond curls firmly.

Grandma looked, Boo thought, as if she had the good sense to be worried.

Cisco carried a last armload of books to the living-room bookshelves from the too-heavy carton in the van. "Grandma, can I—*may* I stick my movie posters up on my wall?"

"Yes, dearie, but only if you can think of a way to do it without marking up the wallpaper with tacks or tape."

Boo took her own carton of clothes and treasures up last. As she did so, she gave a sigh. If only she still had her handmade cardboard model of a movie theater and her witch's costume with the papier-maché hat! The costume had sold for seventy-five cents at their garage sale in Los Angeles, but the model had ended up in the trash can because no one else wanted it. There had been no room for either in the van.

Boo gave another sigh for Susie Loo and Dina Tallman and Nancy Bitts.

Still . . . there *was* her wonderful new room.

It was a pretty room, even if the furniture was old

and the flowered curtains were mended in spots. The rear window looked out across the back gardens to a viaduct and a tree-covered hilltop on the far side of a green valley. Grandma said the bed and rocking chair in the room had belonged to Great-Great-Grandma and Great-Great-Grandpa Smith. The dressing table had been a wedding present to Grandma herself from Grandpa. Boo arranged her seven little glass animals on its top. Her battered copies of *The Lion, the Witch and the Wardrobe* and *Anne of Green Gables* sat in the bookcase beside her father's childhood books and others older still, shabby and interesting-looking.

By early afternoon everyone's everything was unpacked and hung up or neatly put away in chests of drawers with carved decorations and fancy brass handles. Poppy had arranged her paint box, brushes, and carton of crayons neatly atop the low bookshelves between her bed and Babba's in the middle bedroom. Cisco's posters from *The Mark of Zorro* and *Charlie Chan's Holiday* were fastened to the wall of the boys' room. Cisco had used the blue wall-stickum his mother had bought especially for his posters and Poppy's paintings.

Boo dusted and then polished her dresser and chest of drawers and bookshelves in the back bedroom until they gleamed.

Pittsburgh was looking better all the time.

3

Monday Afternoon

"NOW," SAID GRANDMA AFTER BOO AND CISCO AND POPPY had finished washing up the dishes from lunch, "I'm going to bake us a cake for tonight's dessert. How would you three like to trot off to the market for half a gallon of ice cream?" She wheeled her chair across the living room to the bookcase beside the fireplace. Reaching behind the set of encyclopedias on the bottom shelf, she brought out her handbag.

"We'll have our real celebration when your mama comes," she went on. "With decorations and all. Tonight will just be a treat, not a party. After the cake and ice cream you can tell me all about those dreadful Docketts, and I'll tell you tales of the terrible Tuttlebees."

Boo made a face. The Docketts were the sweet-talking couple who, scarcely two weeks earlier, had pretended to be foster parents and had stolen away the four younger Smith children after their mother was taken to the hospital. "It was scary," Boo said.

"And weird," Cisco added. "But sort of fun."

"Only after the happy ending," said Poppy. Poppy did not care for scary adventures.

"Here you are." Grandma held out a five-dollar bill and a sheet of scrap paper on which she had drawn a spidery network of lines.

"I've made you a map and marked the different places where you can buy ice cream in case you'd like to explore the neighborhood. Just don't stray off the map."

Boo wasn't interested in exploring. "It's too hot out. Can't I stay and help with the cake?" Cakes didn't take long to mix. Once the batter was in the pan and the pan in the oven, she could go back up to her room—her own room! She needed to decide exactly where to hang her Best Costume Award certificate from last year's school Halloween parade. Then she might— oh, lie on her bed and read, perhaps, or write a letter to her mother.

"Poppy and I'll go," Cisco offered happily. "I'm a real good map reader."

"Fine," Grandma agreed. "Better take the little picnic cooler on top of the refrigerator, or in this heat you'll be bringing back ice-cream soup. And, I suppose, since it is so hot, you had better treat yourselves to a soda pop apiece. There won't be much change left over, but mind you bring it back."

"Ready?" Grandma asked Boo when the little red light on the stove blinked off.

18

Boo nodded. The batter for the brown-sugar spice cake had been poured into two loaf pans.

Grandma pulled the oven door open. Boo squinted her eyes against the heat and gingerly slid the pans onto the middle shelf. Afterward there was the frosting to make, a special brown-sugar kind that had to be spread on the cakes when they were half cooked so that it could be baked right along with them. Even half done, the cakes smelled delicious.

Danny, who loved cake batter, spent a happy twenty minutes watching the cake bakers, and afterward an even happier ten minutes scraping the batter bowl clean with a finger. Babba preferred frosting, and a spoon for scraping.

"No, I don't like sticky fingers, either, dearie," Grandma said as she handed Babba the icing bowl. "But you miss a lot of the icing with a spoon, don't you?"

Boo grinned as Babba, shaking her head no, pushed open the kitchen screen door and carried the bowl out to sit with it between her knees on the back porch steps.

"Not Babba. She can polish a bowl almost as clean with a spoon as if she stuck her head in and licked it."

"Goodness gracious, Danny!" Grandma exclaimed. "No!"

Boo turned and saw her little brother with his head *really* in the empty batter bowl. Because the large pottery bowl was too heavy for Danny to lift from the table in the breakfast nook, he had stood on the bench

19

and bent down to try what sounded like a good way to lick up the last, spicy smear.

"Stop that this minute, you silly boy," Grandma ordered. "That's my best mixing bowl you're about to bump onto the floor."

"And you've got batter in your *hair*, you goofus," Boo wailed. "You'll have to take a bath before your nap."

The words *bath* and *nap* in the same sentence turned down the corners of Danny's smeary smile. He climbed down from the bench but tucked his chin against his chest, stuck out his lower lip, and wiped his hands on his already sticky, spicy T-shirt.

"Don't wanna nap."

"Oh, yes, you do, Ducky Lucky," Grandma said firmly. "No nap, no cake and ice cream tonight. No bath, only bread and butter for dinner. Boo, you take him up and see he gets a good scrub before he climbs in bed. I'll send Babba up when she's finished scraping her icing bowl."

Danny wriggled away as Boo reached for his hand, but a quick look at Grandma changed his mind. She clearly meant business. Danny, who never butted his head against brick walls, gave a sniffle and followed Boo out into the hallway. Grandma, as she wheeled herself to the hall door, heard him say as he stomped up the stairs, "I *hate* bafs. I hate naps. I hate *you*, Boo."

She heard Boo laugh. "You *love* baths, you goofus."

20

Babba sat motionless on the back porch steps, her sugary spoon frozen in midair. In the patch of tall weeds at the far end of the neglected garden, something had moved. Beyond the two-row garden plot that was all Grandma Smith had managed to plant before the fall that put her in the cast, something moved, stopped, and then moved again.

Babba held her breath for a long moment, and was rewarded at last by the sight of a small whiskered face. She clapped a hand over her mouth to keep from squeaking out "*Kitty!*" in delight.

When Babba's hand moved, the cat stiffened, then vanished into the weedy tangle.

"Kitty-kitty, nice kitty," Babba crooned softly.

Not a weed twitched.

Babba looked at the half-cleaned bowl in her lap. Did cats like icing? Babba loved icing with brown sugar, more even than marshmallow fudge frosting. If she ate two more spoonfuls, there still would be some left for the cat.

Once she had licked the second spoonful clean, Babba carried the bowl to the middle of the lawn. Then she darted back to the porch steps and sat down to wait.

She did not have to wait long. The cat came across the grass at a staggering run. When it reached the bowl it sniffed and drew back with an unhappy *mai-aow*. Then it stretched out a scrawny neck to take a small lick and then, slowly, another. It was not a pretty animal. Its black-and-brown-and-rust-colored coat was dull and matted and looked several sizes too big. Under it, its backbone showed like a thin, sharp ridge.

Babba frowned. Bouncing up from the step, she banged through the screen door into the kitchen.

"Grandma, c'n I have some milk?"

"Of course." Grandma finished drying her cake whisk. She moved across to the cupboard for a glass and then to the refrigerator. "What's the matter, Punkin? Icing too sweet for you?"

"No." Babba shook her blond curls as she took the glass her grandmother held out. "I jus' need some milk."

When Babba reappeared on the porch, carefully holding the glass of milk in both hands, the cat backed nervously away from the bowl. It made a wobbly dash for cover as she came down the steps, but this time it did not disappear. Its wide-eyed small triangle of a face peered out hungrily as Babba took a drink of milk and then poured the rest into the icing bowl. As she backed away the cat came out, putting one foot fearfully in front of the other. Then in a flash, as the screen door banged, it was gone again.

"Good gracious, child! Are you feeding that raggedy little beast from my nice mixing bowl?"

Grandma Smith in her wheelchair, peering out through the screen door, banged the door once again to keep the cat away.

"I know you like cats, Babba, but I don't," she said firmly. "And it's not a good idea to feed them. They come around begging even though they get perfectly good dinners at home."

Babba's blue eyes filled with tears.

"But Grandma, it hasn't got a home. I know it hasn't. It's too awful skinny. *Please*."

Grandma wavered. "Well . . . It does look a bit like a stick in a scrap of fur coat, doesn't it? I suppose just this once won't hurt. But I mean *once*, Miss Barbara Ozma Smith. And you bring that bowl back indoors. We'll put the milk in something else."

In the cupboard beneath the kitchen sink Babba found the old china dog bowl Grandma remembered putting there after Grandpa's and her last dog died. It still had TOBY, the name of Babba's father's long-ago first dog, written on it in chipped red paint.

Back out in the hot, sunny yard, Babba set the bowl of milk on the grass. This time she backed away only a step or two, and sat down cross-legged to wait.

The little cat peered out from under a dock weed. It gave a shiver when it saw Babba, but the milk was too much to resist. The cat teetered across the grass. Spreading its legs wide, it bent its head to lap up the sugary milk. It was so hungry that as Babba inched closer and then reached out to stroke its side, it shrank away for only a moment. The level of the milk fell steadily.

"Don't be 'fraid, kitty-kitty," Babba sang softly as

she stroked. The cat trembled but kept on drinking. "You're *my* kitty-kitty, Cookie. That's your new name, kitty. Cookie-Cookie."

Cookie, under her rough coat, was little more than a skeleton. The fur on her sides and underbelly was matted into flattish clumps. She whimpered when Babba touched her there.

"I'll fix you up 'n' make you pretty. *Then* I bet Grandma will like you."

She reached out with both hands as the little cat licked up the last drop of milk, but the cat was too quick for her. It twisted away, took off across the grass in its odd stiff-legged stagger, and disappeared through the tall lilac hedge along the side of the yard.

Babba scrambled up and dashed for the lilacs. The clumps were crowded close together, but Babba was small and determined. Twigs snagged in her curls and dusty leaves made her sneeze, but in a moment she popped out into the large vegetable garden next door. She was in time to see the tip of the cat's tail whisk through a hole in the fence beyond.

"Cookie! Come back!"

The garden—mostly neat rows of vegetables, with a small patch of grass and a few bushes of old-fashioned roses—was deserted. Babba shot across and, on her hands and knees, squirmed through the same hole under the rotting fence.

"Cookie!"

The little cat was still ahead, making a determined

24

beeline across the back gardens. By the time Babba pushed through a holly hedge into the third garden, shady with apple trees, she was scratched and dusty, with leaves in her hair and a tear in her shorts. An old lady digging weeds under a tree nearby sat back on her heels and watched in amazement as Babba rushed past and into the spirea bushes. A low fence behind the bushes slowed her down a little, but it had slowed Cookie, too. The little cat's wavering run had become an unsteady trot across a fourth garden, one of brick paths and beds of poppies, geraniums, and dozens of other bright flowers.

Babba was sure that Cookie wasn't heading home. If she had a home, she wouldn't be so hungry and skinny. And she was *very* skinny. The hole she squeezed through in the fence beyond the flower beds was too small not only for Babba, but for most cats.

Babba searched, but there was no other way through the fence. At one time there had been other, larger, holes, but each of these was closed fast with sticks and wire or boards and nails.

Babba hurried back to the first hole and, stretching out on the ground, peered through.

The cat was still crouched low under the bush that shaded the hole. It trembled but did not move.

Babba craned to see what it stared at.

A fire was burning in an old washtub. The tub was set up in the middle of a patch of bare earth at the center of an overgrown, weedy back garden. It was a

strange sight on so hot a day. The short, stick-thin
figure who danced around it, throwing in scraps of
paper from a cardboard box, was stranger still. He
was bald on top, with a flyaway fringe of mousy brown
hair. Odder yet, he wore high-top shoes and green
short pants with red suspenders. He hummed and his
knobby knees pumped up and down as he hopped and
skipped around the fire. His elbows flapped. As he
went, he tossed more scraps of paper into the flames.
"Never know, never know!" he crowed.

Just like Rumpelstiltskin! Babba's eyes grew round.

The little cat saw its chance as the dancing man's
back was turned. It began to creep toward the shadows
along the side of the house.

"No, Cookie!" Babba whispered as the cat edged
away. Cookie paid no attention. Instead she cocked
an ear to hear a faint, far-off voice, tinier and even
bossier.

Mew.

A kitten.

Babba sat up in a dither of excitement.

Kittens. Cookie had kittens!

"Oooo—"

Without warning, a strong hand took hold of the
belt at the back of her shorts and hauled her to her
feet. In mid-"Oooh!" Babba's happy exclamation of
surprise became a loud *"Ooof!"* of alarm.

"And just what do you think *you're* doing, missy?"
a gruff voice asked.

4

FROM THE CORNER ABOVE GRANDMA'S HOUSE CISCO AND Poppy crossed to the shade of Oakland Square. In the square, a long, grassy space lined with trees, they sat cross-legged and studied Grandma's sketchy map.

"Here we are, and that's Dawson Street." Cisco pointed from the map to the street that passed the north end of the square. "Look—kitty-cornered right across the street—that's a drugstore and market." At the top of the map, by an X on the line marked *Forbes Avenue*, Grandma had written *Giant Eagle Supermkt*. Poppy thought that was a scary name. *Giant* meant bright, glary lights and dozens of rows of shelves all so long she would get lost just looking for the way out again.

"Where's this one?" Poppy slid her finger along a pencil line to an X marked *Top Luck Market*. "It's got a funny name. Let's go there." The name had a magical ring to it.

The words *Harkness Street* were written along that pencil line.

"Okay," Cisco said. "That's easy. See, Atwood and Harkness and Oakland streets all run the same way. The market we can see from here is at the bottom of Atwood Street, so the bottom of Harkness Street has to be at the next corner along. Right across from us."

Poppy clung to Cisco's hand as they crossed the street. Halfway up the long first block of Harkness Street, he shook free.

"It's too hot to hold hands, silly. Nobody's going to run up and bite you."

Poppy, always timid, began to wish she had chosen the nearer market. The houses crowded along both sides of Harkness Street were like no houses she had ever seen before. Some had peaked roofs like the older houses at home, but these houses were made of brick instead of wooden siding. Most were like brick boxes with windows. Sometimes two—or three or four or five—brick boxes were stuck together. All had porches, some of brick with upstairs porches, too, others wooden, most of them painted in dark colors. A few porches and windows had striped sun awnings, but most windows had their blinds half-drawn against the sun. To Poppy they looked like dark, watchful eyes.

"There's the Top Luck Market."

Cisco cut across the street at an angle. Poppy hurried so close at his heels that she stepped on one of them.

"Ow! That hurt!" Cisco gave a hop, but was too interested in the market to scold. "Wow, lookit that!"

28

The sign that stretched across the front of the Top Luck Market above its blue awning was a bright yellow with TOP LUCK and some words in Chinese writing in red. Around the edges were painted green four-leaf clovers, golden coins, horseshoes, thimbles, and bluebirds. Down the white boards that framed the sides of the doorway, neat lettering read:

FISH	FRUITS
POULTRY	GREENS
EGGS	VEG'S
MILK	SOFT
BEANS	ICE CREAM
NOODLES	ASK IF
BREAD	WE DON'T
SPICES	HAVE IT
CAKES	MAYBE
& LOTS	WE CAN
MORE	GET IT

Inside, live fish swam lazily in a large tank. Smoked sausages from Poland, Italy, China, and Chicago hung from a rafter. The narrow aisles between the shelves were crowded with mysterious packets and boxes and jars and bottles. The labels bore wonderful names like Moon Princess Ginger Powder and Jade Emperor Hoisin Sauce and Celestial Kingdom Oyster Sauce. There were ordinary things, too, like peanut butter and apple juice and Kix cereal and macaroni. At the back there was a refrigerator and freezer section, with frozen dim sum dumplings, plastic bags of frozen squid, and six flavors of ice cream.

Cisco leaned his forehead against the glass window of the ice-cream section. "Oh, boy—chocolate fudge ripple."

"Maybe Grandma doesn't like chocolate," Poppy said firmly. "I think we should get vanilla." Cisco was chocolate-crazy.

"Are you looking for something special?" asked a voice behind them.

The voice belonged to a skinny boy of about Cisco's age and short like Cisco, with dark, bright eyes and straight black hair.

"No, just ice cream," Cisco said. "Only we forgot to ask what kind Grandma likes."

"Vanilla," Poppy said stubbornly, watching the boy shyly. Most boys alarmed her, but not this one. He didn't look as if he would shove or be loud or pull braids. And he was Chinese, like her best friend Rosie Wong at school back home.

The boy gave a slow, solemn nod. "Ah, no. Not vanilla. Strawberry. If today is the twenty-sixth of July and your grandmother's name is Smith, you want strawberry."

Poppy's eyes widened.

Cisco's narrowed. "How'd you know that? How'd you know our name?"

"I guessed." The boy's smile turned into a grin. "Grandmother Smith buys her groceries here. Because she cannot walk now, while your father was away I delivered them to her. She has shown me photographs and told me you would come yesterday, the twenty-fifth. My name is Lee—Lee-Shen Chiang. This is my great-aunt's shop. And you—you are Francisco Moonlight Smith and Poppy Luisa."

Cisco blushed. "Just Cisco," he put in quickly. He hated his goofy middle name, but couldn't get rid of it. It kept popping up like a pesky gopher. "I guess we'll have half a gallon of strawberry, then."

A soft voice came from behind them. "Why not a quart of strawberry and one of vanilla? Your grandmother has chocolate sauce. Lee delivered it to her last week."

The children turned to see Great-Aunt Chiang, a neat, plump little woman with gray hair drawn back into a bun. She wore a flowered dress and apron and a pair of tinkly gold earrings and shook hands with each of the children as Lee introduced them.

"I see you have a map, Cisco," Great-Aunt Chiang said. "Lee, we're not busy now. Why don't you give Poppy and Cisco a soda pop and show them some of the neighborhood so they'll know where places are? I can phone Mrs. Smith to tell her you're off on a tour. If you leave the picnic cooler here, you can decide about the ice-cream flavors when you come back."

It was much too hot to go far, but Lee showed Poppy and Cisco the Jewel of Bihar restaurant up the street,

31

and on Atwood Street the hardware store and gift shop and little restaurants. Then they headed back toward the market. Lee talked nonstop all the way.

". . . and a lot of people rent rooms to students from the universities. The University of Pittsburgh is only two streets away, you see. There are students there from all over the world. My Uncle Joe—his Chinese name is Yao-Lung—he is studying to become an engineer."

When Lee paused to take a breath, Poppy spoke up quickly.

"Lee? Where do you come from? You talk funny. Different, I mean. Not like your aunt."

"Great-Aunt is an American," Lee said. "My father and mother and Uncle Joe and baby sister Lily and I came from Hong Kong only two months ago to live with Great-Aunt. My father sent money to buy the building next door, but not long after we came, we found out that Mr. Fazio, who sold us the building, did not own it. We cannot open our restaurant after all, so my father works as a waiter at the Golden Pagoda downtown."

They reached Harkness Street and turned back toward the Top Luck Market.

"Did your dad get his money back?" Cisco asked.

"Not yet."

Poppy stopped unexpectedly.

"What is it?" Cisco turned to give his sister a sharp glance. She looked a bit wilted from the heat, but not the pasty-pale color that meant she was feeling woozy.

"I don't want to go in there," Poppy whispered.

"The market? Why?" asked Lee.

Poppy pointed.

Cisco gave the market another look and recognized the cart parked by the screen door. It was shaded by a purple umbrella. Old Mrs. Tuttlebee's cart.

"She's not going to bite you," Cisco said impatiently. It was, after all, their first chance for a good look at the Wicked Witch close up. How could Poppy not be curious?

Lee seemed less sure. He shook his head solemnly. "You never know. Mrs. Tuttlebee is very strange. She *might* bite. Or snap. Poppy can wait here if she wishes, and we will bring the ice cream out."

The boys vanished into the market before Poppy could decide whether or not Lee was making a joke about Mrs. Tuttlebee biting.

Cautious Poppy's bump of curiosity was not very large, but she did have one. Bit by bit it drew her near enough to peer into the cart. Except for a grimy small-animal cage, its contents were a few disappointing odds and ends of junk. The cage, half covered by a sheet of old newspaper, appeared empty. Then, even though Poppy had not touched the cart, the cage gave a tiny lurch and tilted sideways under the newspaper.

Poppy gave a squeak as she jumped away. Swiftly she retreated to the sunny corner of the house next door. Once her heart stopped thumping she found herself yearning for a quick peek under the newspaper—and for the shade beneath the Top Luck Market's awning. But she didn't dare. What if old Mrs. Tuttlebee came out and thought she was snooping? Perhaps when Cisco came out, *he* would sneak a peek.

Too late!

The Wicked Witch suddenly popped out onto the sidewalk like a trap-door spider after a fly. The market's screen door banged shut behind her. She slung her plastic shopping bag into the cart, knocking the cage onto its side. Perhaps it was empty after all.

The old woman peered down the street, across, and up. Spying Poppy frozen against the porch next door, she scowled and then chuckled. The chuckle was even scarier than her scowl. Still chuckling, she pointed a bony finger at Poppy and sang in a scratchy voice, "Goggle eyes, goggle eyes / What if they turned froggle eyes?"

Then she was gone. When the boys came out, Poppy was still staring after her.

Cisco was carrying the picnic cooler. "What are you doing clear over there?" he asked.

Lee smiled. "Mrs. Tuttlebee didn't bite after all," he told Poppy. "But she did growl at Great-Aunt for not having any orange-blossom tea."

Poppy took a deep breath. "I saw her," she said, afraid to say anything more for fear the boys would laugh. Instead, she turned and took off across the street. Cisco gave Lee a wave and followed.

Half a block from the Top Luck Market a long-legged young man jogged past the children. A little farther on he slowed to a stop to wait for them. He wore shorts, a tank top, and a baseball cap.

He fell into step beside them. "I know you," he said. "You're the Smith kids. I saw you unloading your van this morning. I'm Peter Quilty. I live next door to you at Mrs. Finnerty's, so I know your grandma. Which Smiths are you?"

"I'm Cisco. This is Poppy."

Poppy, who had turned to peer back the way they had come, looked at the young man warily.

Cisco was cautious about talking to strangers, too, but he didn't want to be rude to a neighbor. Peter Quilty *looked* okay. His hair under the cap was red and curly, his pale skin freckled, and the backs of his arms and legs and shoulders were bright red with sunburn. Besides, they had almost reached Dawson Street and were only a short dash from Oakland Square, Hillyard Street, and Grandma's house.

Peter Quilty saw Cisco eyeing his sunburn and grinned. "I fell asleep," he explained. "I was out in the back garden yesterday reading a deadly dull law book. I fell asleep and got fried."

"Poppy always gets fried," Cisco observed. "That's why she has to wear the hat. And tops with sleeves."

Poppy, who had craned around again to look back up Harkness Street, turned pink with embarrassment.

"Wise woman." The young man nodded gravely. "If I had worn a shirt and hat I wouldn't have to pretend that blisters are cool."

Poppy smothered a giggle. She liked words that played games with each other. Cool blisters!

Peter peered at her curiously. "Tell me, Poppy, is your head on a swivel, or are we being followed by suspicious characters?"

Cisco took a look back up the street himself.

"*I* don't see anybody."

"It was that spooky old lady at the store," Poppy answered in a small voice. She had felt sure that the Wicked Witch and her rubber-wheeled cart were creeping up behind them, but she was not going to say so. Cisco would only snort and call her silly.

"Spooky? Mrs. Chiang?" Peter's eyebrows lifted.

"Not her." Cisco shook his head. "The old lady who lives down the street from Grandma. Mrs. Bumblebee or something. She really *is* weird. Guess what she was buying—fish eggs and *snails*. Snails in a can!"

"That's Mrs. Tuttlebee, all right. Weird from word one," Peter agreed with a grin.

Poppy frowned. "She had funny stuff in her cart. There was a broken flowerpot and a bunch of old wire hangers. And a pan lid and some broken plates. But the—"

"It figures." Peter snorted as he led the way across Dawson Street. "Stingy old bat! A friend of mine from law school rents the attic room in her house, and just about everything in it's patched up or wired together. Nothing matches, not even the legs on the table. I wouldn't worry about the old lady's sneaking up be-

36

hind us, Poppy. She's probably poking her way home down one of the alleys, checking out the trash cans before the garbage truck comes around tomorrow."

They walked along under the trees that bordered the northeast side of Oakland Square.

"Are there lots of people at Mrs. Finnerty's where you live?" Cisco asked.

"Not as many as there are Smiths. Our house is smaller. Old Mr. Havlichek's in the downstairs front room, and Mrs. Finnerty has the two rooms on the next floor. Yuri Ivanov and I are up on the top floor. Yuri was a dentist in Russia. Now he's studying to take the exams so he can work on American teeth, and nights he works at whatever job he can get. We hardly ever see him. Right now he's a janitor. He—" Peter broke off. "Hey, looks like you've got company."

He pointed.

The children looked across to where Hillyard Street's short length dipped downhill from the side of the square. Down in Grandma Smith's tiny front garden a stout, red-faced man in a silver-blue shirt and blue-and-white checked trousers was hammering a sign on a stake in the middle of the rose bed. Even from thirty yards away the three larger words on the sign stood out clearly.

The two in black letters were FOR SALE. The third, in fat red letters, was pasted slantwise across them.

It read SOLD.

5

"WHAT MAN? WHAT SIGN?" GRANDMA SMITH WHEELED herself to the front screen door and peered out. "In *my* rose patch?"

"Right here." Cisco, in the tiny front garden, grasped the sign and wrenched it around on its metal stake so that his grandmother could see it. Below the SOLD sign it read, LASS & TEMPKIN, REALTORS. CALL 555-8713.

Boo, curious to find out what all the fuss was about, came up behind Grandma's wheelchair. When she spied the FOR SALE sign and the SOLD sign pasted over it, she went as pale as vanilla pudding.

"Oh, *no!*"

"Mercy me, if that doesn't beat all!" Grandma exclaimed. "Whoever he was, he didn't even ring the doorbell to make sure he had the right house. Peter, will you pull it up for us? I'll phone the real estate people. They'll have to come collect it."

"Is it really—" Boo cleared her throat. "Are you sure it's a mistake, Grandma?"

Grandma Smith wheeled around to face her. "Of course I'm sure, dearie. It's my house. If I'm not selling it, it can't be for sale, now can it?"

Peter Quilty was clearly curious, but after he had uprooted the sign from the rose bed, he handed it to Cisco, then gave a wave and moved on. He turned in at the house next door.

Cisco passed the ice cream in its cooler to Poppy and lifted the sign to carry it indoors. Boo held the screen door open.

Grandma was waiting in the wide living-room doorway.

"That's right, dear," she told Cisco. "In the corner behind the door. And you, Poppy—you scoot along and put that ice cream in the freezer."

"*Ice* cream? Can I have some?"

Babba popped into view on the hall stair landing. She wore clean clothes and was still damp-looking from the scrubbing Boo had given her in the bathtub after she was hauled home by grumpy Mr. Havlichek from next door. Mr. Havlichek also took care of the garden four doors down, where he had caught her.

Danny, rubbing his eyes, appeared behind her.

"Not till after dinner, Babba, dear," Grandma said. "But you and Danny *can* come help me find some important papers I need before I phone the real-estate people."

The children hurried down the stairs.

"Cisco, I had a *'venture*," Babba announced as she

came. "There's a spooky house an' a little man with a wooden leg an' Cookie's baby kittens. Cookie's my new cat."

"Is not," Grandma said gruffly. She wheeled herself across the living room to the desk in the corner by the front window. "No cats! Now, Danny—can you open the bottom drawer for me?"

Unlike Babba, who had cuddled up to Grandma from the start, Danny was still a little shy of this grandmother-stranger. Even so, like Babba, he did love opening other peoples' drawers to see what he could see.

"Careful, dearie," Grandma warned. "It's a very heavy drawer. If you pull it too far, it'll fall out and squash your toes." She watched as Danny, a chunky, strong little boy, tugged at the drawer's handle with all his weight. Babba helped by tugging at the waistband of Danny's shorts.

"There, that's far enough," said Grandma. "Thank you, gumdrops."

The children stared at the metal box that fit snugly inside the drawer. It was gray and solid looking.

Cisco came to watch. "Wow, it's a safe!"

"No, dear, just a fireproof strongbox to keep important papers in. But it's very heavy. We'll need Boo to—" Grandma looked around. "Now, where has that girl got to?"

"Upstairs," Poppy said. "To her room, I s'pose."

"Poppy?" Babba pulled at her sister's shirt. "I had a 'venture. I saw—" But Poppy was listening to Grandma.

"No matter," Grandma said. "Cisco can probably shift the box far enough back in the drawer for Babba to fit the key into the lock. Here's the key, Babba." To Poppy and Cisco she said, "I want to get out the deed for the house so that you can see it truly *is* ours. Every penny paid. I know you had a very upsetting time after you lost your home in Los Angeles. I want to show you that you don't have to worry about *this* house."

Poppy tapped on Boo's bedroom door at the back of the third-floor hallway.

"Go away!" came the muffled answer.

Poppy opened the door a crack and peered inside.

Boo sat in Great-Grandma's rocker, not rocking, just sitting stiffly. She held an old book with a grayish green cover and the title *The Submarine Chums*, but she wasn't reading. She hadn't gone back to looking miserable as she had all the way from California to Pennsylvania. Instead, she looked frightened. That was scarier.

"Your room's really nice," Poppy offered timidly after a moment's silence. "Don't you like it?" Poppy really wanted to ask, "What's the matter?" but she always felt safer edging up on feelings sideways.

"It's okay," Boo said, but the way she hugged herself as she looked around showed that she thought it was a lot better than okay.

Poppy was puzzled. "Then what's wrong?"

Boo bit her lip and blinked. Then suddenly the words tumbled out in a rush. "I just bet you that FOR

41

SALE sign's not a mistake at all. It'll be like all the times when I was little. I know it will. Every time a place gets to feel really like home, something horribilous happens and we have to move again. What if—what if Grandma forgot to pay her taxes or something and the county or city or whatever has sold the house to pay what she owes? We haven't got anyplace more to move to. And what about when it's time for Mama and the new baby to come? Or winter. What'll we do then?"

Poppy sighed. Boo was always cheerful enough when she was busy, but when she didn't have something to do or a book to read, she started imagining. If she wasn't daydreaming about everything being all silk cushions and chocolate cake, she was worrying about what dreadful thing might happen next.

"Don't be a goop. How can anybody take Grandma's house away? It's all paid for. She's got the deed for it downstairs. We saw it. It's stamped CERTIFIED and it's got an official seal and the date. She has a mortgage paper that's stamped PAID, too. She showed them to us just now."

"Honest?" Boo bounced to her feet. "Poppy, I could hit you! Why didn't you say so right off?" She hurried into the hall, where she almost ran smack into Babba.

"Boo, listen," Babba began eagerly. "I had a 'venture 'safternoon. I saw—"

"Not now, Babba." Boo dashed past and down the stairs.

"Poppy, listen—"

42

"Later, Babby, I promise." Poppy ducked around her little sister and followed Boo.

"Nobody answers," Grandma said testily. She banged down the telephone receiver. "Only one of those phone machines. It says that their office hours are ten to four. It's only five minutes to four, and already they're all out the door. Dratted nuisance!"

"Who's a nuisance, Mom?" The front screen door slammed shut behind Mr. Smith, who appeared in the living-room doorway.

"Those pesky real-estate people. They stuck a FOR SALE sign smack in the middle of my roses," Grandma answered. "You're home earlier than usual."

"I caught the first bus this time," Mr. Smith said. He opened and began reading with a frown a letter he had picked up from the little pile of mail on the hall table. After a moment he looked at the envelope again as if to make sure that it had come to the right house.

"What is it, Dan?" Grandma asked.

He looked up grimly. "These letters addressed to Dad that came while I was in Los Angeles—what on earth do they mean?" he asked. "This one's from Keystone Savings and Loan in Wilkinsburg. Giving us notice the house is up for sale! On top of that, they're billing us for two months' overdue rent! And this other one's a 'Landlord-Tenant Complaint' from the municipal court, directing us to pay back rent and damages and get out of the house. What in blazes is going on?"

6

MR. SMITH HEADED FOR THE PHONE. "FOR PETE'S SAKE, Mom, why didn't you show me the letters as soon as we got in last night? Or this morning?"

Grandma threw up her hands. "I forgot. They came week before last. I knew they were nonsense. A mistake. I forgot all about them until the children showed me that SOLD sign. That gave me a start, but it *is* a mistake. You know it is."

"I know and you know. The court doesn't seem to," Mr. Smith grumbled as he riffled through the phone book to the *K*s. "That notice gave us ten days to notify them we mean to fight the eviction."

He looked at the postmark again. "Ten days from the twentieth. That's—this Thursday! I'll have to get a letter in the mail tomorrow. We'll be lucky if it gets there in time." He dialed the number for the Keystone Savings and Loan Company.

After a brief conversation Mr. Smith hung up and announced, "They're open till five. If we hurry that'll give us time for a quick stop at Qwik-Copy to make photocopies of the deed and mortgage papers. Boo, you'd better come with Grandma and me."

Boo didn't want to go. All she wanted to do was flee to her room, fling herself onto the bed, and wail into her pillow. She could hardly say that, though. At every excuse she came up with, her father shook his head. She wasn't needed to baby-sit—the younger children could go to Mrs. Finnerty's. If she really had a head-ache, Grandma could give her half an aspirin. Her bedroom wall would still be standing in an hour and a half even if she didn't hang up her costume award that very minute. She had to go. Period. Tomorrow or some other day Grandma might need to take a taxi to the court building in downtown Pittsburgh while Mr. Smith was at work. Boo would have to go along then to help with the wheelchair and hold doors open, and all that would be easier if she had a practice run.

Boo sulked all the while she and Grandma waited in Elvira outside the Qwik-Copy shop and most of the way to Wilkinsburg. Who on earth needed practice opening doors? It was only when she noticed how tightly her father gripped the steering wheel, and the nervous way he chewed at his lower lip, that she realized he was frightened, too. They had arrived at the Keystone Savings and Loan building twenty minutes before closing time, and while they waited outside the manager's office, he held her hand so tightly that her fingers began to go to sleep.

45

The manager, a sandy-haired man wearing a gray suit and a tie with tiny flying ducks on it, greeted Grandma and Mr. Smith with handshakes and a broad smile. The broad smile was replaced a few moments later by a look of sorrowful sympathy as Grandma told him about the mistake and showed him the copy of the deed.

"Yes, Mrs. Smith, but six months ago you signed a grant deed transferring the property to Mr."—he checked a paper in the file folder on his desk—"Victor Woller."

Grandma sat up straight as a poker and looked him in the eye. "I did no such thing."

"Now, Mrs. Smith, you've just forgotten. Most of us do grow forgetful as we grow older. I'm sure your son understands that and won't blame you if there are business matters you've let slip or not kept record of."

Grandma glared. "I keep excellent records."

Mr. Smith looked calm, but Boo could tell from his voice that he was angry. "Mother always looked after the family finances," he said. "She was a department-store bookkeeper before she was married. At Horne's."

"No, at Kaufman's, dear," Grandma whispered.

The manager held up his hands. "I'm sure you were an excellent family money manager, Mrs. Smith, but we are talking about today. You're what—seventy-nine? Eighty?"

"Seventy-five," snapped Grandma.

"Seventy-five. And being looked after by your son, which is as it should be. You mustn't fret yourself about these little lapses of memory. We—"

Boo's temper began to simmer as she realized that under the sugary words, the man was saying that Grandma was soft in the head. Grandma!

It was Mr. Smith's turn to hold up a hand. "Excuse me, but my mother doesn't even have to make grocery lists. Her memory's better than mine."

The manager's smile grew thin. "Perhaps so, but the fact remains that the property was recorded in Mr. Woller's name in January. According to the records he provided when he applied for a mortgage in February, he paid eighty-five thousand dollars for the house, and after that you were paying him a monthly rent of five hundred dollars. That means you owe us one thousand dollars for the two months since we took over the property. The new owners, who bought the house at auction on Saturday—"

Mr. Smith interrupted again, more loudly this time. "You don't seem to understand. "*Mom* owns the house. She never sold it. Period."

The manager placed the tips of his fingers together. "No, Mr. Smith, *you* don't understand. We made a loan on the property in good faith. The deed to the property is at present still registered in our name. We have clear title to the property."

Boo almost bit her tongue. It's not "a property," she wanted to yell. It's *home!*

"And now," the manager continued smoothly, "if you will excuse me, it's past closing time."

The three middle Smith children were sitting with Peter Quilty on the porch steps of Mrs. Finnerty's house next door. On the porch itself, gray-haired Mrs. Finnerty sat in her wicker rocker, shelling peas for supper into a bowl in her lap. Old Mr. Havlichek, a tall man with gnarled hands, thick white hair, and a face as wrinkled and almost as brown as a walnut, sat with Danny on the wide porch swing.

"An' he was just like Rumpelstiltskin," Babba said, her eyes still wide. But no one was listening.

"Is that where your gran and your dad went roaring off to half an hour or so ago—the savings and loan company?" Mrs. Finnerty asked Cisco over Babba's head.

"And Boo." Cisco nodded. "Daddy wanted to get copies made of all the deeds and stuff first and go to the bank after work tomorrow. But Grandma was mad enough to spit tacks. She wouldn't wait. She says nobody's going to steal *her* house. Boo went with them so she'd know how to work the wheelchair and stuff if Grandma has to take a taxi down to the court building tomorrow."

"An' he had a wooden leg," Babba said loudly.

"A taxi?" Mrs. Finnerty pooh-poohed the idea. "As if Alice Smith needs to hire a taxi when Gus's old rattletrap is sitting right out front just collecting dust."

"Rattletrap?" Gus Havlichek's bushy white eyebrows shot up. "She's no such a thing!"

Cisco and Poppy turned to look at the battered green sedan parked at the curb.

Peter Quilty grinned. "C'mon, Gus. Admit it. She looks more like a Dodgem car than a Dodge."

"What's a Dodgem car?" Danny asked.

Mr. Havlichek snorted. "She's a classic, that's what she is. Nineteen fifty-seven, no less. I may decide to sell her one of these days, but like I always say, it's handy havin' her around."

He gave the swing a little push as he explained to Cisco and Poppy. "M' driver's license ran out last month, and they told me they couldn't give me a new one. I'm ninety years young and fit as a fig tree, but I guess the old eyes aren't up to par. Still, young Peter here can drive her. Your grandma won't need any taxi."

Danny pulled at Mr. Havlichek's shirt. "Hey! What's a Dodgem car?"

Babba eyed the empty space on the swing, but she had not yet forgiven Mr. Havlichek for scolding her for trespassing in other people's gardens. She gave a sniff and the little toss of her head that made her blond curls bounce. "My grandma doesn't need any old green car. She likes taxis because they're yellow. And they've got lights on top."

Mrs. Finnerty looked as if she were trying not to smile. "My, you are full of it, aren't you, dearie?"

49

Babba's brows drew together. "Full of what?"

"Silly pudding," Cisco answered, giving her a warning nudge.

"WHAT'S A DODGEM CAR?" Danny roared.

Mr. Havlichek gave a loud hoot and laughed until he got the hiccups. He had to go indoors for a drink of water. Danny looked from Mrs. Finnerty to Poppy to Cisco to Peter and wondered what everyone was laughing at.

Peter recovered first and explained.

"A Dodgem's a—a game-ride at a fair or park. Big kids or grown-ups with little kids get to drive little cars with fat rubber bumpers. They chase each other around and dodge and go bump-bump-*bump*!"

Danny laughed. "*I* wanna go bump. Can we go to the Dodgem today?"

"Not today," Mrs. Finnerty said. "I suppose there's a Dodgem at Kennywood Park. I haven't been there for thirty or forty years. When the weather cools down a bit, we could all go. It might be fun."

Mr. Havlichek had reappeared at the screen door. He snorted. "Feels like it's never going t' cool down." To Danny he said, "Tell you what, shorty—I've got something for you to do right now. Tomorrow, anyhow. You can give me a hand in the garden out back. I got a lot of weeds to pull out, and you're a lot nearer the ground than I am. Penny a weed. Is it a deal?"

"Deal!" said Danny.

"Shake on it," said Mr. Havlichek, and they shook hands.

Peter looked up toward the square. "Hey, here come your folks."

The old van pulled up in front of Grandma's house and the children ran to meet it.

As the front passenger door opened, Cisco cried, "Is that bank place really trying to steal your house, Grandma?"

"*Are* they?" Poppy chimed in anxiously.

Boo was scowling and Mr. Smith wore a worried look. Not Grandma. Grandma looked red-in-the-face angry enough to start whistling like a teakettle.

"Maybe not them, but *some*body sure as succotash is," she snapped.

7

Monday Evening

BOO DISAPPEARED INTO THE HOUSE LOOKING LIKE A SMALL, dark thundercloud. Grandma, once Mr. Smith had pulled her wheelchair up the two steps onto the Smiths' porch, wheeled herself over to the side railing and poured out to Mrs. Finnerty and her lodgers the tale of her attack on Keystone Savings and Loan.

". . . and would you believe it? They say I sold my house to this Victor Whatnot—"

"Victor Woller, Mom," Mr. Smith said.

"Willer, Waller, Woller! The name doesn't matter a pin. Neither your dad before he died, nor I, sold any house to Victor Anybody, ever."

"Keystone says they gave Mr. Woller a mortgage six months ago," Mr. Smith explained. He rubbed his forehead as if it ached. "They loaned him fifty thousand dollars. When Woller stopped making the payments, they foreclosed. They put the house up for auction last week."

"I bet Mr. Woller is a crook," Cisco said eagerly. "I bet you Woller's not his name at all."

Mr. Smith sighed. "Cisco, this is serious. You're not Sherlock Holmes and this isn't some old movie of *The Case of the Purloined House.* I don't want to hear any wild theories. I still think the whole thing's some gosh-awful mistake. The only other possibility, Mom, is that either you or Dad signed some kind of agreement without reading the small print. A roof-repair contract. Something like that."

Old Gus Havlichek gave a gloomy nod. "It can happen. Before I moved down here twenty or so years ago I had a room up on Harkness Street. This roofing company claimed my landlord missed a couple of payments on his new roof. He said he hadn't done any such thing, but the roofers took him to court. Said he'd signed some paper that let them sell the house to get their money if he didn't pay up. And by gum, they did it! The law let 'em sell the house right out from under him."

Poppy went pale. Cisco leaned forward intently.

Grandma Smith nodded. "That was poor old Frank Corso, wasn't it? He was a friend of my papa's. As best as I can recall, some other folks got stung, too. The company was—Rufus Roofing! That sticks in my mind because their truck used to park just down the street here."

"Yes," Mrs. Finnerty agreed. "That awful little Rufus man rented a room for a while down at Tilly Tuttlebee's."

"But—Mr. Corso got back the *rest* of the money from his house being sold, didn't he?" Poppy asked in a small voice. "After the roof got paid for?"

"Well, yes and no, missy," Mr. Havlichek answered. To the company in general he said, "There was something tricky about the paper he signed. All he got was the five thousand dollars he paid for the house in nineteen twenty, but it sold for thirty-five thousand. Wasn't long before Frank was flat broke. Had to move in with his son somewheres up Turtle Creek way."

"Yes, yes. All that's neither here nor there," Grandma Smith put in impatiently. "I haven't signed a blessed thing. Granddad didn't either, and it's a good ten years since we had the roof fixed. Tomorrow I just may go downtown to see whether I can get some sense out of the folks at the Recorder of Deeds Office. And I'd like to give the real-estate people a piece of my mind, too. Never mind. Right now I've got dinner to see to."

Poppy went to hold the screen door as Mr. Smith pulled Grandma's wheelchair up over the threshold into the front hall.

Babba got up from the step, dusted off the seat of her shorts, and followed. "Daddy," the others heard her say as the screen door banged, "*you* want to hear 'bout my 'venture, I bet."

Mrs. Finnerty frowned. "Now I think of it, that's happened more'n once hereabouts even after Rufus the roofer took off ahead of the police. Folks losing their houses, I mean."

"Honest? How many times?" Cisco asked eagerly. "Dozens?"

"Dear me, no." Mrs. Finnerty stripped her last pea pod and began to scoop the empty pods into a plastic shopping bag. "Let's see: There was Elsie Gemelli eight or nine years ago, over across the square. Elsie kicked up a royal fuss, said the paper she signed was for a loan for storm windows, all right, but she never got the windows."

Poppy blinked. "What are storm windows?"

Mr. Havlichek grinned. "Never been in a real winter, have you? They're just glass or plastic windows in a metal frame. You fasten 'em on the outside window frame in wintertime to help keep the cold out."

"Seems to me," Mrs. Finnerty went on, "there was some newspaper reporter who got interested in Elsie's problem and nosed around a bit, but a fat lot of difference all the fuss made. Poor old Elsie!"

She rose to carry her peas into the house. Mr. Havlichek brought the swing to a stop.

"Reckon I'll go take me a shower before supper." He pulled himself to his feet with the help of the swing's chain. "Toodle-oo, one and all."

Poppy drifted down Mrs. Finnerty's porch steps and back to Grandma's house. Cisco stayed put. Fumbling in his shorts pocket, he brought out a pencil and a little spiral notebook fastened shut with a rubber band. He found a blank page and began to write.

"How do you spell *Gemelli*?" he asked Peter.

"G-E-M-E-L-L-I." Peter Quilty grinned. "What's that, Sherlock? Your detective's notebook?" He reached over and tilted it so he could see. The name *Frank Courso* headed a new page, and below it was written, *Elsie G.*

Cisco's cheeks burned redder than the sun had turned them. "Well, it *is* a mystery. At least Grandma's house is."

"Uh-huh." Peter scratched his chin. "I wonder . . . the Bhallas and Ritters, over across the street. They're being kicked out of their apartments. It doesn't figure. Their landlord, old man Potnick, he's off in a nursing home. Angie Bhalla says he's gaga. Doesn't even know his own name. So *he* can't be the one who's kicking them out. I wonder . . ."

Cisco was writing furiously. *Balla. Ritter. Potnik.* After a moment he added *Changs restarant.*

When Boo came downstairs after tucking the two smallest Smiths in for the night, Mr. Smith was in the kitchen washing up the supper dishes with Poppy and Cisco drying. Grandma sat in her wheelchair at the kitchen table, reading the evening newspaper.

Boo was still grumpy from the upsetting—and wasted—visit to Keystone Savings and Loan.

"Phoo!" she said. "Putting Danny to bed's like trying to tuck in a slithery lizard. And Babba—Grandma, you better watch out for Babba. There'll be kittens all over the house if you don't sit on her quick."

A smile erased Mr. Smith's gloomy look. "I take it that Cookie, the cat in Babba's 'adventure,' was real even if the dwarf with the wooden leg and the grumpy giant weren't."

"A dwarf with a wooden leg?" Grandma laughed. "The story gets better every time the child tells it! The grumpy giant, though—that's Gus Havlichek. He found her in the Petersons' garden and hauled her home. The cat she was after was a straggly, scrawny-looking beast. Probably full of germs. I hope she didn't touch it."

"Your grandma," Mr. Smith explained to the children, "doesn't like cats. One ate her pet canary when she was Babba's age, and she's never forgiven 'em. Cookie hasn't got a chance."

Neither Poppy nor Boo looked convinced.

Grandma changed the subject. "Boo," she said, "my mind's made up. Tomorrow you and I'll go down to the City-County Building to the Recorder of Deeds Office and the Deed Registry. Tess Finnerty'll look after the little ones again. When I phoned to ask her, she said Peter could drive us in Gus's car. Peter doesn't have any Tuesday-morning classes."

"If he's going, why do I have to?" asked Boo.

"Because," said Grandma shrewdly, "I think the more you know, the less you'll fret."

"Okay." Boo made a face. "The people tomorrow better be nicer than that man at the loan company, though. He didn't even *listen* to you, Grandma. The way he talked, all they care about is getting back all the money Mr. Woller tricked them into loaning him, no matter what. It's not fair."

Mr. Smith sighed. "That's what they're paid to care about. Look, let's not talk about the house anymore. And I'll write that letter to the court tomorrow morning, not tonight. I want to be able to get to sleep and dream about brown-sugar spice cake and your mom, not wicked bankers gloating and twirling their mustaches. Besides, it'll all straighten itself out. You'll see."

Cisco knew his father was serious about having no house talk. He wore his too-tired-to-think look even though he smiled and tried to sound jokey. He had already pooh-poohed the idea that the wrangle over who owned Grandma's house was a swindle. "A misunderstanding," he called it. Mr. Smith liked to look for the simplest explanation for everything.

Cisco, on the other hand, itched fiercely to be asking questions. If he couldn't ask any at home . . .

"Daddy, when we finish the dishes, can I go up to the Top Luck Market?"

"At this hour? No, Cisco, you may not." Mr. Smith looked at his watch. "It's past seven o'clock. I know it's light until nine, but what on earth do you want that won't wait until morning? It can't be candy. Not after two helpings of cake and ice cream."

"I don't want to buy anything. I just wanted to go see Lee Chiang."

"Lee—? Oh, Mrs. Chiang's nephew's boy. I'm sure

he'll keep until tomorrow. Look, the rest of these dishes'll dry themselves. Why don't you three go in and watch some TV? Aren't the "Star Trek" reruns on at seven?"

"That's back home in California." It was hard to stop thinking of California as home.

"So, check the listings in the newspaper," his father said shortly. Being reminded that Mrs. Smith was still in California and stuck there for another six weeks or more always made him either gloomy or grouchy. "Grandma's not reading that section. Better still, go read a book."

Cisco and Poppy spread the page with the TV listings out flat. To their surprise Pittsburgh had almost as many TV channels as Los Angeles. Even so, nothing looked interesting. And the rerun of "Star Trek: The Next Generation" was already over. In Pittsburgh it came on at six o'clock, not seven.

Cisco decided instead to go look for a book to take out onto the front porch. It was still light, and a little cooler outside now that there was a bit of a breeze.

He found the perfect book in the living-room book-case. It was an old paperback with a worn green cover and pages yellowed and brittle at the edges, but it was exactly right. His father's name, Danny Smith, was on the inside of the cover. The title was *The Young Detective's Handbook.*

8

Tuesday Morning

MR. SMITH GOT UP EARLIER THAN HIS USUAL SIX O'CLOCK
to write a letter to the clerk of the court that had sent
the eviction notice. He made it short and clear: "Yes,
we will fight the eviction. My mother, Alice Winkler
Smith, owns the house free and clear. Neither she or
my late father, Daniel Smith, Sr., sold it or any share
in it. If either signature is on the Woller deed, it is a
forgery. Yours truly, Daniel Smith, Jr."

"It feels good to do *some*thing," he explained to
Grandma and to Boo, who had come down early for
breakfast. "If I can get home early enough this afternoon, we'll go find out what the people at that real-
estate office can tell us."

He licked the flap of the envelope, stuck on a stamp,
and looked almost cheerful as he left for work.

Tuesday was a flop all around.

"I was wrong about the Bhallas' landlord," Peter
Quilty announced at nine-thirty that morning when he
answered Cisco's knock at Mrs. Finnerty's screen

door. Cisco was there to tell Peter that Grandma Smith and Boo were almost ready to come out to the car. Poppy, Babba, and Danny would be coming over to Mrs. Finnerty's in a minute.

"Wrong how?" Cisco asked.

"Oh, the Bhallas are still getting kicked out." Peter picked up Mr. Havlichek's car keys from the hall table and joined Cisco on the porch.

"They're still getting kicked out, but old man Potnick himself is selling the house. At least, his nephew out in California is. The Bhallas say the nephew took charge of his uncle's property and taxes when the old man started to lose his marbles. Now Mr. Potnick's nursing-home fees are bigger than his pension, and the medical bills have gobbled up his savings. So it's the house's turn to go. It ought to bring enough to last him."

"Couldn't it be somebody pretending to be his nephew?" Cisco asked hopefully. If Mr. Potnick wasn't being swindled, that left only Grandma and the Chiangs' next-door neighbor, Mr. Fazio. And Cisco wasn't sure of him yet.

"Nope. Sorry, Sherlock. The Bhallas know young Potnick. They talk to him on the phone once a month, after one of them's been out to the nursing home to visit the uncle." Peter looked up to see old Mrs. Smith start down the porch ramp in her wheelchair. "Oops, we'd better open up Gus's car. Here comes your granny."

61

While Boo struggled to fold up the wheelchair, Peter lifted Grandma Smith and neatly slid her onto the backseat of the big, old Dodge. She sat sideways so that the seat was wide enough for her to stretch out the leg with the cast, with room to spare. Peter lifted the wheelchair into the trunk, Boo climbed into the front passenger seat, and they were off.

So was Cisco.

Poppy, holding hands with Babba and Danny as she climbed Mrs. Finnerty's front steps, watched Cisco go. His shoulders were back, his hands in his pockets, and his most serious detective-chief-inspector frown in place. Even in shorts and thongs and with a sunburned nose, he looked thoroughly businesslike. Poppy was sure he was right. There really *was* a mystery, and now he was off to dig up notebooks full of facts and sniff out all sorts of clues.

She sighed.

It was very hard being eight years old and nearly as short as five-year-old Babba. Everyone forgot she wasn't a baby too. Being short didn't mean you couldn't help with detective work. Cisco and Boo were short, too, weren't they? Short for ten and twelve, anyway.

Poppy knocked on Mrs. Finnerty's screen door.

The day went downhill from there.

Grandma, Boo, and Peter left for downtown at half past eight. At both the Recorder of Deeds Office and the Registry of Deeds they found that a deed for the house on Hillyard Street *had* been filed and registered by a Victor Woller. No one in either office could remember, after six months, what he had looked like. As for his address, he had given only 519 Hillyard Street, Grandma's house. "The nerve of the man!" Grandma had fumed.

Cisco struck out, too. Lee Chiang had gone with his father to look at a restaurant advertised for rent in the morning newspaper.

Babba trapped Cookie in the garden shed Mr. Havlichek and Grandpa Smith had built between their two vegetable plots. Cookie got away when Babba tripped over a hoe and scraped her knee.

Danny went out to help Mr. Havlichek weed Mrs. Finnerty's garden. Before Mr. Havlichek came out of the shed to start his this-is-a-weed lesson, Danny had pulled up a bean bush, six young parsnips, and an onion.

Poppy helped Mrs. Finnerty make brownies. The chocolate she took down from the cupboard turned out to be the unsweetened kind, not the semisweet the recipe called for. The brownies were not a success.

Mr. Smith came home from work with a limp. A new truck tire he was lifting into place had slipped and struck his shin as it fell. It had left a painful bruise.

Wednesday *had* to be better.

9

Wednesday

ON WEDNESDAY MORNING MR. SMITH LEFT FOR WORK AT SIX o'clock as usual.

At nine Boo, Grandma, Peter, and the old green Dodge started out for the office of the real-estate agents, Lass and Tempkin.

Cisco headed for the Top Luck Market.

Poppy sighed and took Babba and Danny to Mrs. Finnerty's for the morning.

Two hours later there was a banging at Mrs. Finnerty's screen door. A cheerful voice called, "Peter! I found it!" When there was no answer, the voice rang out more loudly. "Come on, Quilty, where are you? Mrs. Finnerty! Is *any*body home?"

Babba and Danny were in the back garden with Mr. Havlichek, learning how to tell tomatoes and carrots, squashes and peas, and beans from weeds. Poppy was stretched out on the living-room floor, reading an old strip cartoon book called *Mutt and Jeff in the Trenches*. Mrs. Finnerty was in the kitchen.

"Poppy," Mrs. Finnerty called. "That's Peter's friend Nancy. Tell her he won't be back till lunch." Poppy moved shyly to the door.

"I heard," the young woman on the porch said. "Hi. I'm Nancy Wheat. Who are you? And may I come in?"

"I'm Poppy," Poppy half whispered. "Just a minute." She turned and fled back along the hall to the kitchen.

"Mrs. Finnerty?" she said breathlessly. "She wants to come in. Is it all right? Should I let her in?"

"Of course, dearie." Mrs. Finnerty stirred away at a large kettle. "Tell her I'm out here, up to my elbows in jam."

When Poppy unhooked the screen door, Nancy Wheat strode in. She wore sandals and a sleeveless blue dress. Her hair was pulled back into a blond ponytail under a baseball cap. She carried a book bag slung over her shoulder.

"Poppy? Smith, I'll bet. Right? Where's Mrs. F.? In the kitchen?"

Poppy nodded dumbly and followed as Nancy breezed back along the hallway and stuck her head around the kitchen door. She sniffed.

"Red currant! Smells great. Look, Mrs. F., I've got a book for Peter. He wanted it in a hurry, so I told him I'd zip into the library after my nine o'clock class. Where shall I leave it?"

"The hall table's as good a place as any."

As Nancy vanished, Mrs. Finnerty said loudly,

"Come by this afternoon, if you like, and you can have a jar of jam."

Nancy dropped a fat book on the hall table. Poppy saw that its title was *Property Transactions*.

"I will," Nancy called back. "Now, if Mrs. Tuttlebee handed out treats like you do, I wouldn't be all skin and bones."

There was a cackle from the kitchen.

Poppy stared. "But you're not skinny."

"Just a joke." Nancy laughed. "Mrs. Tuttlebee's my landlady. She wouldn't give a cat-crunchie to a starving relative."

Poppy's eyes widened. "You live at the Wicked Witch's house?"

"Is that what your grandma calls her?" Nancy's eyes twinkled. "She *is* sort of spooky. Her house is pretty spooky, too. Have you seen it? It's the one down at the end of the street."

Poppy shook her head. She had been curious, but not curious enough to go exploring without Boo. Or Cisco.

"Does Mrs. Tuttlebee have a pet?" she asked.

"A pet?" Nancy shrugged. "Not that I know of. At least, I haven't seen or heard one. I suppose she might have a cat that stays indoors. Hang on—yes, she must have one! I remember seeing a cat-crunchie bag in the trash can once. I just never thought about it before. Why?"

"I looked in her cart the day before yesterday. Outside the market. There was a cage in it, like something to put a little animal in."

Nancy smiled. "And you thought if she had a cat she might have kittens to give away? To you?"

"No." Poppy shook her head. "Grandma doesn't like cats. I just thought maybe—maybe she's mean to it. Maybe she doesn't feed it enough." She was thinking about Cookie. The house in Babba's adventure had to be Mrs. Tuttlebee's. Poor Cookie!

Nancy nodded. "Tell you what—next time I put my trash out, I'll do a quick snoop through hers to see whether there are any more cat-crunchie bags or boxes. If there are," she added, "I'll look for cat-food tins, too. It's not healthy to feed cats just crunchies."

Poppy blushed. "Thank you." She drifted after Nancy as she opened the screen door and crossed the porch.

Nancy stopped, then turned to smile down at her. "Would you like to see a bit of Tottering Towers, Poppy?"

Poppy stared blankly.

"Mrs. Tuttlebee's house," Nancy said. "Tottering Towers is what Peter and I call it. Would you like to take a quick peek? It will have to be a quick one, because I have a lot of reading to do for my afternoon class."

Poppy gave a shiver of excitement mixed with dread. "Oh, yes! I'll go ask Mrs. Finnerty."

* * *

Mrs. Tuttlebee's house was even stranger than the awful Docketts' creepy house in Los Angeles. Its shingled walls weren't covered with ivy and it wasn't surrounded by a tall fence, like the Docketts', but—like the Docketts'—it did have tall trees all around it and a thick, prickly hedge, and turrets on top. *Five* of them. The Docketts had had only two. And the Docketts' house had been shabby, but not downright rickety. Some of Tottering Towers's shingles were missing, and the entire house needed a coat of paint. In a few places traces of the old brown paint could still be seen, but everywhere else the house was the weather-worn gray of bare wood. Mrs. Tuttlebee's front porch looked as if it might fall off the next time anyone sneezed at it.

Tottering Towers stood at the very end of the street, where the hill fell away steeply down toward the park in the deep, wide hollow below. To Poppy the house looked as if it were leaning away from the edge of the hill, tilting back as if it were itself worried about teetering on over. From the street it was impossible to see any part of the downhill side of the house except the turrets. The uphill side was hidden behind a hedge of tall, shaggy pine trees and the next-door fence. In front, an overgrown barberry hedge pushed its prickles out over the sidewalk to snag and hold passersby. Hold them for eating, Poppy found herself thinking. Like a Venus's-flytrap plant. She shivered. The face of the house looked as unfriendly as the Wicked Witch herself. The curtains on its windows all were drawn. A sign tied to the gate set midway along the front hedge read NO TRESPASSING—KEEP OUT—THIS MEANS YOU!

Poppy slowed.

"I better not go in," she said hurriedly. "I forgot, I promised Mrs. Finnerty I'd help her stir the jam."

"Don't worry," Nancy said. "You're with me. Besides, no one's here. On my way home just now I passed Mrs. Tuttlebee. She and her go-cart are somewhere up past the Chinese market by now. And I see Mr. Zimmerman, her downstairs tenant, go out every morning before eight. He's as regular as a clock. Honest. I promise."

She opened the iron gate—which gave an alarming screech—and waved Poppy in ahead of her. Poppy went, but her feet felt as heavy as if she were wearing iron boots instead of the old tennis shoes her mother had painted with pink and red poppies.

"Oops, no, not the front door." Nancy caught at Poppy's arm to pull her onto a side path bordered with weeds. "Around this way."

The path led around the corner of the front porch, past the trash cans, and into a shady aisle between the house and the row of pine trees. There an outdoor stairway stepped steeply upward to a landing. From the landing it turned and clung to the side of the house itself until it reached the attic.

Beyond the foot of the stairs, the space between the tree trunks and the next-door neighbor's fence looked like a rubbish dump. Stacks of rotting firewood and a heap of old lumber leaned against the fence. Broken trellises, a wheelless wheelbarrow, rolls of rotting tar paper, and ancient window screens full of holes were piled against them. There was even—strangely—a rusty old farm plow. Everything was covered with dust and decorated with spiders' webs.

Nancy and Poppy climbed the stairs. Several steps up they passed a dirty window. The curtains behind it were firmly shut. Just below the landing they passed a second dirty window that had no curtains at all, except for a large and dusty cobweb. Squinting, Poppy could make out several dark, framed pictures stepping up the opposite wall above a climbing stair rail, and a wide strip of peeling wallpaper.

"Yuck!" Poppy wrinkled her nose. "Why do you live in such an awful house?"

Nancy laughed. "Because it's cheap. And I have my part all to myself."

On the landing she gave the wall of the house a tap.

"Mrs. T. keeps saying she's going to have a door put in here so her other lodger won't have to come and go through her part of the house. She won't, though. She's too stingy to spend money."

"What's a lodger?" Poppy asked nervously. She was trying hard not to look down through the spaces between the wooden steps. The ground was uncomfortably far below.

"It's a roomer. Someone who rents a room in your house. Like Mr. Zimmerman. He keeps pretty much

70

to himself." She grinned. "All I see of him is the top of his head from my front window when he goes out in the morning."

Nancy reached the top landing and crossed a short wooden walkway that led to a door in one of the round roof turrets. She unlocked the door and pushed it open. "Here we are! Come on up."

Poppy clung to the stairway's stout wooden railing. The landing three steps up was higher than the roof's eaves. The walkway to the door crossed several feet of steep shingled roof with no safe, solid wall beside it. Poppy's knees and courage wobbled. The ground was much too far below. She shut her eyes, but that made her dizzy, so she opened them quickly.

Baby! she told herself. Baby, baby, baby!

No. Worse than a baby. Babies would go—at least the Smith ones. Danny would clamber up and charge across without even looking down if he thought there was ice cream beyond the turret door. For a kitten, or a chance to snoop inside somebody's house, so would Babba.

"I'm coming," Poppy quavered.

She did it by holding on to the railings on each side and fixing her eyes on the chair just inside Nancy's door. Then she put one foot exactly in front of the other, heel touching toe, heel touching toe. Suddenly she was inside, and everything was fine.

Nancy's room was large, with a high, raftered ceiling that went up to a peak in the middle, but only three small windows. The walls needed fresh paint and the

71

furniture was a collection of shabby odds and ends, but Nancy had brightened it with cushions, lamps, a flowered spread draped over the sofa, and posters on the walls. Without them the room would have been a dark, spooky attic. For a kitchen, Nancy had an electric hot plate, saucepan and coffeepot, and a little tabletop refrigerator.

Poppy peered out of a dormer window into the tidy next-door garden below. There was no window overlooking Mrs. Tuttlebee's back garden, but from the turret window on the far side of the room she could look straight down into the tops of trees growing on the steep hillside. In one nearby tree she saw what looked like the roof of an old tree house. Across the deep green hollow, large buildings—the university?—nestled among trees atop the far rim of the hollow.

"Look around for a minute more if you want," Nancy said. "I've got to hit the books. Big test tomorrow." She unloaded her book bag onto the table, opened a book, and sat down to read.

Poppy wavered. After a moment she said, "I guess I'll go back."

Nancy looked up. "Okay. Next time you come, maybe I won't have to work. I'll get some soda pop. D'you like cherry?"

Poppy felt almost as wobbly going down the stairs as going up. On the bottom step she hesitated. The sooner she was outside the gate, the better, but she was curious about the cat. Remembering what Nancy had said, she headed for the trash cans beside the path at the corner of the house.

The trouble with trash cans was that they held smelly, squishy things. Poppy lifted the lid of the first one and almost dropped it. Her nose wrinkled. She would not touch the wet paper sack on top in case it held fish heads or something worse. Beneath it she spied a shoe, a broken bottle, and what looked like a bundle of old clothes, but no cat-food cans or empty crunchie bags. In the second can, on top of a jumble of newspapers, a sack had broken open and spilled out what looked at first like a dead mouse in a paper cup.

Poppy squeaked and dropped the lid with a clatter as she backed away.

"*Whuzzat?*"'

Poppy froze.

The voice had come dimly from somewhere inside the house. It was followed by the muffled sound of approaching footsteps.

Poppy looked around frantically for a place to hide.

The nearest window was higher up than she was tall. If she squatted down beneath it she would be out of sight, but only if the owner of the mysterious voice and footsteps did not open the window. In a panic, she made a dash for the stairs up to Nancy's room. Ducking behind them, she found a narrow space between a heap of rotting firewood and a stack of old fruit crates.

There she crouched down and hid her face against her knees.

The first sound was the groan and rumble of a sash window being forced up. Then Poppy heard a snort and grumble. But if both Mrs. Tuttlebee and her lodger were out, who was in the house?

"Dratted dogs!" A man's voice.

Poppy didn't dare peek. When she heard the window slam down again, she waited as the footsteps died away. Even then she did not move for several minutes. When her heart finally stopped thumping like the big drum in a marching band, she took a deep breath. A slight breeze rustled in the pine trees overhead, and the only noise was the faint hum of distant traffic.

And a sad, thin, kittenish *mew*.

Babba was right. There *were* kittens.

Or at least *a* kitten. A hungry one, too, from the woeful sound of it.

Poppy crept back along the side of the house, but the sound did not come again. There was not a tail or whisker of kitten to be seen.

But there, suddenly, was Cookie.

The little cat was headed back along the side of the house. Poppy followed without thinking. A moment later she found herself kneeling on the half-rotten step of a ramshackle screened-in porch. The bottom of the door had only a few shreds of screen left. What looked like a large cupboard or chest of drawers had been shoved up against it to block the entrance, but years of rain and winter weather had buckled and split and rotted loose the cupboard's plywood back. Much of its bottom section was gone. Cookie had vanished through the opening.

Poppy peered inside. Except for dust and grime, she saw only a battered enamel bowl with a rusted-out bottom and a ratty old basket. Beyond the basket, one of the cupboard's lower doors stood ajar. Paw prints across the dusty cupboard floor showed that Cookie went that way often.

Curiosity proved too much even for cautious Poppy. One small peek couldn't hurt. With the bowl and basket pulled out and both cupboard doors pushed open, Poppy leaned in to peer at the porch itself. It was dark not only because of the trees crowded along the fence—bamboo blinds hung along the screen walls, and cardboard boxes were stacked high in front of them. On the end of the nearest carton Poppy could make out a cat's face and a word that looked like *Purr-something.*

Cases of cat food?

In a moment Poppy had crawled into the cupboard to take a closer look. As she did so, a cup hook screwed into the underside of the shelf just above snagged her T-shirt. Poppy froze in alarm. It mustn't tear—it was green with pink polka dots, and her best. Wriggling and shrugging, she moved sideways and back until she could reach the hook with her hand. Once the T-shirt was freed, she was so anxious to make sure it hadn't been torn that, before she knew it, she had scrambled on through and out the cupboard doors. Pulling her shirt around, she saw that the hook had left a grimy smear, but no hole. When she realized that she was inside, standing in the shadowy porch, she wavered, half frightened and half amazed. The frightened half wanted to scramble out again as fast as hands and knees would take her. The amazed half could only stare at what it saw.

The porch was both a storehouse of bundled newspapers and a treasure house of food. Food for cats. Food for people. Mouth-watering food. Mysterious food, peculiar food. The tall stacks of cartons were all cases of canned goods: half a dozen sorts of cat food; and for people, whole button mushrooms, giant olives, smoked oysters, fancy salmon, *rattlesnake* meat, baby asparagus and carrots, tiny potatoes, Danish hams, strange wrinkled mushrooms labeled *Morels*, and much more. Some cases had holes cut in their ends so that cans could be taken out; many were untouched. Poppy stared, as wide-eyed as if she were Ali Baba and the porch the robbers' treasure cave.

Beside the doorway from the porch into the house itself, a case of apricot nectar sat on top of four others. There was strawberry ginger ale, condensed milk, strawberry cream soda, and fizzy water from France. Beside them, the door stood ajar.

Cookie, nowhere in sight, must have gone on into the house itself. Poppy shivered. Poor Babba—Cookie really *was* the Wicked Witch's cat.

Poppy itched to see what was beyond the door, but she was as frightened as she was curious. Her hand went out to the doorknob, then was snatched back.

Thump!

The sound was small, and soft, as if it came from somewhere far off, but Poppy backed away from the door in panic. When the door moved, she almost squeaked aloud. Then she saw Cookie. The little cat nudged once again at the door, then lowered her head to pick up a dark object from the floor. Without even a glance at Poppy she flashed past, headed for the cupboard. She ran with her head held high, carrying a fish too large for such a small cat.

Poppy dove for the cupboard, too, but by the time she had scrambled out, Cookie had vanished once again. Poppy's hands trembled as she reached in to pull the cupboard doors nearly shut. She pushed the old bowl and basket back into place and smeared away a handprint she had left in the dust. Then she took a deep breath and tiptoed back toward the trash cans.

If only there were a gate—or a hole—through the fence to the next-door garden! Poppy dreaded the eight or so yards from the corner of the house out through the gate in the front hedge. The house had at least eight or ten front windows. What if at one of them a hand were to pull a curtain aside and suspicious eyes peer out? The scary question wouldn't go away: If both Mrs. Tuttlebee and her roomer were out, who had come to the window to grumble about dogs and garbage cans?

When she reached the trash cans, Poppy picked up
the fallen lid and moved gingerly to replace it, then
paused to frown at the dead mouse in the plastic cup.

It wasn't a mouse. It was a mustache.

10

LEE CHIANG, UNPACKING A CARTON OF LITCHI NUTS AND
stacking the jars neatly on a shelf, was puzzled.

"But Cisco, what can your grandmother's—what do
you call it?—her 'pickle'?—have to do with the failure
of Father's plans for the building next door?"

"Maybe nothing," Cisco admitted. "But didn't you
say your father found out the guy he was buying it
from didn't own it after all?"

Lee nodded. "Mr. Fazio. He has lived in the house
for as long as Great-Aunt remembers. For more than
forty years. When Great-Aunt came to America to
marry Great-Uncle, Mr. Fazio and his wife had a restaurant there. When Mrs. Fazio died he closed it. He
is very old now. Eighty, perhaps."

"But what about the house? The loan company says
Grandma doesn't own hers anymore because she sold
it, but she *didn't*. Why doesn't Mr. Fazio own his?"

Great-Aunt Chiang, counting out change to a stout,
red-faced woman in a sleeveless flower-print dress,

looked up. "What's that?" she exclaimed. "Is it true, Francisco? Your grandmother has had a bad-news letter from the bank?"

Cisco nodded. "Day before yesterday," he said. "But it wasn't from her bank. It was from some old Keystone Savings and Loan Company."

The red-faced woman, halfway to the door, turned to waggle a fat finger at Mrs. Chiang. "I told you right from the start there was something fishy going on next door. Now, didn't I?"

Great-Aunt Chiang wore an unhappy frown. "Yes, you did. But the bank that claims to own Mr. Fazio's house—the First Commonwealth Bank—is old and well respected. I was sure it would not set out to cheat an old man. And he is forgetful sometimes. I thought perhaps he had signed loan papers and then forgotten. . . ."

"Hah! Don't you believe it," the red-faced woman scoffed as she opened the screen door. "Tony Fazio never lost track of a penny in his life."

When she had gone, Cisco said glumly, "I dunno. Since it's not the same bank or whatever that took both houses, I guess it's not a plot after all."

"Plot?" Great-Aunt Chiang gave him a puzzled look.

"Yeah. It would have been a great one—houses getting stolen all over the place." Cisco sighed.

"*Chut!*" Great-Aunt Chiang was thoughtful. "Don't be so quick to lose heart, Francisco. Aren't two mysteries—two terrible mistakes or two villains—twice as good as one? The court has told poor Mr. Fazio he must be out of his house by this Friday. Perhaps you can learn something from him that will help your grandmother."

Lee nodded eagerly. "I will take you to meet him as soon as I have restocked the shelves."

"Finish the condiments," Great-Aunt Chiang said briskly. "The rest can wait until later. I begin to think that there may be more questions we should have asked Mr. Fazio. Once we learned the house no longer belonged to him, we could have tried harder to find out how he lost it. You see, when Mr. Fazio didn't have a lawyer to advise him at the court hearing, we thought that was because he had remembered that the bank was right after all. But perhaps he couldn't afford one. We never asked that. We were too busy worrying about when—and perhaps whether—we would get our deposit back. You go ask your questions. It may not be too late."

"I'll be only a minute," said Lee. He ripped open the last of the condiment cartons. "I have only the hoisin sauce left to put out."

Mr. Fazio's living room was tidy but very dusty. The furniture was old-fashioned: overstuffed chairs with lace doilies to protect the arms, and dark, varnished tables, magazine rack, and bookcases. Cardboard cartons were arranged in a neat square in the center of the flowered carpet. One was half-full of books. Another held a tall pepper grinder and a small frying pan. The rest were empty.

Mr. Fazio himself was stoop-shouldered and balding, with a neat mustache and thick-lensed eyeglasses. Even though the house was almost as hot as the morning outdoors, he wore a sleeveless pullover sweater over his shirt and woolly slippers on his stockinged feet.

"Alice Smith is your grandma? And she has had an eviction letter, too?" Mr. Fazio was bewildered. "I don't understand. I would think her mortgage was paid up many years ago, like ours. September of nineteen fifty-nine ours was paid for. That day my Gina and I, we have a party in our Ristorante Roma downstairs, and everybody drinks toasts to us with the sparkling wine."

The old man smiled, remembering. "We pour grappa on the mortgage paper and burn it in a chafing dish. It was a good party."

Cisco fidgeted on his chair.

Lee was not so shy. "Please, sir—how long ago did your letter from the bank come?" he asked.

"How long ago? Two months, I think." The old man frowned. "No, not two months. Six weeks maybe."

Lee was surprised. "Just before Father and Mother and Uncle Joe and Lily and I came from Hong Kong!"

Cisco was dismayed. Five or six weeks! Grandma would be upset when she heard that. That wasn't much time at all. And now, since it was already Wednesday morning, Mr. Fazio had only two days left before he would have to move out. It was scary. Sherlock Holmes or Charlie Chan or Lieutenant Columbo might be able to solve mysteries in a day or two, but Cisco Smith? When he didn't have a single clue to work with, only a hunch?—a hunch and the fact that it was all more unfair than—than—well, than *anything*.

What was it *The Young Detective's Handbook* said? "Ask the right questions, and the clues will follow."

Cisco thought for a moment and then asked in a small voice, "How long after they warn you do they tell you when you have to get out of your house?"

Old Mr. Fazio gave a pale smile. "First they let you have your say, if you wish. When I answer the letter, they name a court date for the next week. In court I tell the judge I wish to sell the house and go back to Italy, but I never yet sign the deed paper over to anyone. I tell him I never hear of this Mr. Sidney T. Ullman they say has bought the house from me. But the judge says the *Antony Fazio* on the deed paper looks just the way I sign it. Since I cannot prove it is a forgery, the law is clear, he says. The loan company, they give Mr. Ullman his mortgage in what is called 'good faith.' When he does not always pay on time, they worry. Because the house is good, in a nice location, the bank buys the house loan from the loan company also in 'good faith.' But then Mr. Ullman stops making his payments. The house, therefore, the judge says, now belongs to the bank to sell. Everyone's word is good, you see, but mine!"

Cisco chewed at his thumbnail for a moment.

"That Mr. Ullman—did you ever see him before?"

"Him? Hah! I *never* see him. And he was not in the court." Mr. Fazio flapped his hands. "Not he! Six-seven months ago he takes his who-knows-how-many thousands of dollars from the loan company, makes one, maybe two payments on the house loan, and then is gone. *Fsst!*"

Cisco's heart beat faster. That was what the people at the Keystone Savings and Loan had told Grandma about Mr. Woller, wasn't it?

"Did you ever sign any kind of paper, sir? Like, for ordering a new roof, or storm windows?"

Mr. Fazio shook his head firmly. "No. Not a one. I know never to sign papers from salesmen who come to the door. That is what is so puzzling."

Lee spoke up. "My father says you should have had a lawyer, sir."

Mr. Fazio shrugged. "Who has money for a lawyer? I have only enough to take me back to Italy. I have nephews and cousins there. But you must tell your father his money is safe. It is in the bank, in a savings account. On Friday, when I must give up hoping, I shall return the money to him."

Lee brightened, but then caught himself and tried, politely, not to look too cheerful. "That is good news for my father, sir, but I am sorry, too."

"Mr. Fazio?" Cisco crossed his fingers. "Did you ever hear about anybody else's house getting stolen? Around here, I mean."

"Here in Oakland?" Mr. Fazio frowned and smoothed his mustache. "No-o. But you see, I do not go out much. I would not hear."

He saw the boys' disappointment. "Aha!" he exclaimed. "Of course! I understand now why so many questions. You are not simply curious young busybodies. You are snoops in earnest. Detectives detecting! You are thinking that if my Mr. Ullman and Francisco's grandmother's Mr.—"

"Mr. Woller," Cisco prompted.

Old Mr. Fazio's dark eyes gleamed. "If Mr. Ullman and Mr. Woller are the same man, then there may be more of him, eh? Is that it?"

At Cisco's nod the old gentleman heaved himself up out of his chair and began to pace the shabby flowered carpet. As he went, he tapped a finger at the side of his mouth.

"So little time! Let us see—who would know of other such thieveries? My good friend Rudy Jakowsky? No, he is a cardplayer, but not a talker. We require a true collector of news and tittle-tattle, a 'nibby-nose,' as my Gina used to name them. Umm. Hannah Tobey? No, she goes last year to live with her daughter in Atlanta. Poor daughter! Umm. Bernie Coogan? He is not so good at remembering nowadays. Hah!—Florrie Gallo. Florrie would know. From five blocks away Florrie would know how many sausages you ate for breakfast and that it was the O'Briens' cocker spaniel that barked in the middle of the night. Yes, you go ask

Mrs. Florence Gallo over on Semple Street about lost houses. She will know."

Mrs. Florence Gallo had not lived in the house on Semple Street for several months. The woman who answered the door sent Cisco and Lee off to ask at St. Agnes's Church, seven blocks away. Father Hughes at St. Agnes's sent them trudging off to the Trimble Nursing Home on lower Dawson Street. At least the nursing home was on the way home for Cisco. Sort of. The home was an elderly frame hillside house, freshly painted a neat gray with white trim. Perched partway down the Lower Oakland hill, it was near the opposite end of Dawson Street from Oakland Square. Its neighbor on the uphill side, where two pale, grubby children dug in the dark earth under a maple tree, badly needed a coat of paint. So did several on the downhill side. Their shabbiness made the nursing home look as tidy as a dollhouse with seven men and women, some black and some white, sitting stiffly on the rocking chairs on the porch.

Old Mrs. Gallo turned out to be a frail, birdlike little creature hunched over in a wheelchair in the home's TV room. Most of the oldsters glumly watched television or dozed in their chairs, but Mrs. Gallo's dark eyes twinkled and snapped and her tongue was sharp as a knife.

"Tony Fazio? That old bucket of gloom's still alive?

And he sent you to see me? Why? What are you up to? If this is some silly adopt-a-grandma-for-the-summer project, save your breath, kiddos. I'm not available. Too wobbly."

But Mrs. Gallo's memory, once Cisco and Lee had explained themselves, was not at all wobbly. *She* had lost *her* home, she explained as she led the boys into the front living room. An official letter from a bank in Greentree that claimed to have taken over a Mr. Oscar Pennyman's mortgage on the house had come "like a bolt out of the blue." Then, only days before the court hearing, she had a small heart attack and landed in the hospital. The eviction had gone on without her.

"Pooh!" Mrs. Gallo waved a hand. "I'm fine now. Better every day. And madder'n hops! Why, yesterday I got another bill from some storage company where the court's marshals or constables or whatever they call themselves took all my furniture and doodads. Well, they can whistle for their money! Let 'em keep the rugs and tables and chairs. I haven't got a floor to put 'em on, and I can do without the doodads."

Sitting back in the wheelchair, she raised her voice. "I'm not the only one, either. The same thing happened to Lucy Bridger over there. Kicked out of her own house, she was, same as me!"

Mrs. Gallo beckoned to a woman across the room, who rose and limped toward them with the help of a cane.

Cisco scribbled *Lucy Brigder* in his notebook.

Mrs. Bridger settled into the armchair nearest Mrs. Gallo. She was a stout, gray-haired black woman in a daisy-print dress. When Cisco asked about her house and how she had lost it, she gave a sigh.

"That's right. It like to broke my heart. That was the house Mr. Bridger and I lived in close on to sixty years. It still makes me boil! If I had that limb of Satan, Mr. Marvin Nissler, here right now, I'd tie him up like a rolled pork roast and make him listen to a good, sharp sermon. With maybe a wallop or two for sauce."

Marvin, Cisco wrote. He looked up. "Nissler?"

"That's right. N-I-double S-L-E-R." Mrs. Bridger smacked the floor with her cane with each letter.

"What did Mr. Nissler look like?" Lee asked.

"Bless you, child, I never laid an eye on the man."

Cisco and Lee exchanged an excited look.

"Mr. Nissler, he didn't come to the court hearing," Mrs. Bridger explained. "But that judge—he believed him anyway. He believed I signed Mr. Nissler's deed paper, and I did no such a thing!"

Mrs. Gallo leaned forward in her wheelchair. "It's not just us, neither. There was Pat O'Dea, for one. Poor Pat, he just dried up and died once they took his place away and his nephews moved him in here last month. He'd say, over and over again, 'I'm sure glad Mary Frances isn't alive to see this day.' Why, he built that house for her with his own hands, every brick, back after the nineteen eighteen war."

Mrs. Bridger gave an indignant cluck. "Man forged a sale paper and deed for it," she said. "Then he borrowed money on it and skedaddled. Same as happened to us."

Five houses! Five houses all in the last few months. Cisco was almost hopping with excitement. Now his father would have to believe it was a plot. With villains!

Lee's dark eyes shone. "Did Mr. O'Dea know the man's name?"

An elderly black man who wore a tie and long-sleeved shirt in spite of the heat had come in from the porch and stopped to listen. "Kenneth something," he put in. "Larrimore? I'm afraid that when Patrick spoke of him, his language was extremely . . . startling. But I think that was the name."

"But he never met this Larrimore, Reverend Sanders," a new voice put in. "The dirty rat lit out before all the fuss."

Turning, the boys saw that another old man and several of the women had come in from the porch.

Cisco, puzzled, looked around the circle of faces. "But—I don't understand. If you all knew the houses were stolen, why didn't you call the cops?"

"We did," said several of them together.

11

CISCO AND LEE LOOKED AROUND THE LITTLE CIRCLE. "SO? What did they say?" asked Cisco.

One old man snorted. " 'Tough luck!' That's what they said."

"Now, Frank," Mrs. Gallo said, "that's not fair. If you mean that nice lieutenant who came down here to see me, he said the cops knew it was pretty suspicious when 'new owners' disappeared into thin air. They couldn't get a line on any of 'em. Anyhow, he said the real trouble was, once the court said our houses weren't *our* houses, there wasn't much the cops could do for us. Except they'd still keep an eye out for my Mr. Pennyman and the other skunks."

Cisco's heart sank.

"Ah," said the Reverend Sanders, "but these two young men are going to turn something up." He leaned forward. "My guess is you're onto something new already. Am I right?"

Cisco looked around the eager, anxious circle of faces, and his heart sank even further.

*   *   *

At lunch twenty minutes later, Cisco scowled at Poppy over his bologna sandwich. "Why would I want somebody's ratty old Halloween mustache?"

"For a disguise," said Poppy. "I thought detectives use disguises. They *do*. There's a chapter about them in your detective book. I know 'cause I saw it."

"Oh, sure." Boo looked up from her lunch to scoff. "A ten-year-old kid with a mustache. That'd be a great disguise."

"Detecting's hard work, not fun and games," Cisco said, trying to look grown-up and serious. "The book says more'n eighty percent is legwork—asking questions and taking notes. 'Often you must open bushels of clams before you find even a tiny pearl,' " he quoted.

"Clams?" Poppy looked confused.

"Grandma," Danny announced loudly, "guess what? I pulled threety-two weeds."

No one paid attention.

Poppy's cheeks had flushed pink. She seemed very interested in twiddling her fork around in her apple-and-raisin salad.

"I just thought you *might* want it," she told Cisco meekly. "Anyhow, I left it in the trash can."

"I should think so!" Grandma exclaimed. "There's no knowing whose sniffly nose it's been pasted under. *And* no telling what kind of germs it was full of. But what I want to know is what on earth you were doing in Matilda Tuttlebee's trash can in the first place."

91

"How much money is threety-two cents?" Danny demanded loudly.

"A quarter, a nickel, and two pennies," Boo said. She pushed his apple-juice glass closer. "Drink your juice, goofus. It's not polite to interrupt."

"I bumped the can and the lid fell off," Poppy said in answer to Grandma's question. She explained about Nancy's invitation to visit the attic apartment. She told about the mysterious man who came to the window, too, and about seeing Cookie go into Mrs. Tuttlebee's house. She left out the part about the porch, though, and what she saw there. It had been wrong to snoop. She really did want to tell, but what if Grandma made her go down to apologize to the Wicked Witch for breaking into her house—even if it was only the porch? Just thinking about it made her insides feel shivery.

"You saw Cookie?" Babba was so excited that she almost slid off the cushion that made her tall enough for the table. "She runned away after I brought her some milk for breakfus. Where'd she go to?"

"Well—" Poppy said reluctantly, "I saw her go into the Wicked Witch's house."

"Ah!" Grandma sounded relieved. "So it *is* Matilda's cat. I must say, it's a shame she doesn't feed the poor thing better. Even so, Poppy, you really shouldn't call her 'the Wicked Witch.' It's unkind, and it was naughty of me to tell you that's what some folks call her."

Babba was indignant. "Cookie's not her cat. She's *not!*"

92

Boo changed the subject hastily. "Grandma and I went to the real-estate office this morning. I guess that's what Cisco calls 'legwork.' Only we didn't find out anything to take notes about. About all they said was, the savings and loan company hired them last Saturday to arrange an auction to sell our house and two others. So they did."

"What about you, Mr. Almost-Late-to-Lunch?" Grandma asked Cisco. "You came dragging in as if you'd run all the way from here to Harrisburg and back. What were you and Lee Chiang up to all morning? More 'legwork'?"

Cisco made a silly cross-eyed face. "We sure were!"

By the time he had finished the tale of Mr. Fazio, Mrs. Gallo, Mr. O'Dea, and Mrs. Bridger and their houses, Grandma was sitting up in her wheelchair straight and stiff as a lamppost. Her eyes shone with excitement.

"Holy smoke, Cisco!" Boo was impressed. "*Five* houses? You were right all along, then. Even if, like Grandma and Mr. Fazio, they say they didn't sign any papers for the crooks to use. It *has* to be a plot."

Babba giggled at the "holy smoke." Grandma looked as if she might get up and dance, hip cast and all.

Boo reached out her hand for the notebook, and when Cisco handed it to her, read down through the last list of names and dates.

Grandma—last week—Victor Woller
Mr. Fazio—5 weeks ago—Sidny T. Ullman

93

Mrs. Gallo—June 7—Oscar Pennyman
Mrs. Brigder—6 weeks ago—Marvin Nissler
Mr. ~~Oday~~ O'Dea—May 23—Keneth Larrimor

Five houses in two months? It really *was* too much for coincidence.

"Great!" Boo exclaimed. "Just wait'll Daddy gets home. I bet he takes you to show this to the cops. They'll *have* to go after the bad guys now."

Grandma beamed at Cisco, but then her smile gave way to a small frown. "Why so glum, Cisco dearie?"

He shrugged. "The cops already know. They told Mrs. Gallo the court said all those houses were sold, not stolen, so the police couldn't do anything. They said she could get a lawyer and peel what the court said—"

"*App*eal," Grandma said. "It means going over the court's head to a higher court."

"Anyhow, they said it'd be pretty hard for her to prove Mr. Pennyman swindled her when nobody could find him. They got his description from the loan company, but it didn't help."

Grandma sighed. "That's the way it was eight or nine years ago, too, when those storm-window salesmen cheated so many folks. And about twenty or so years ago that Mr. Rufus, too—the roof man—*every*body knew what he looked like, but he packed up, drove off, and—poof! Nobody ever saw him again." She sounded as discouraged as she had been excited moments earlier.

"Well, we can't quit," Boo said defiantly. "Nobody's going to steal *my* room if I can help it. Like Daddy says, doing something at least makes you feel better. Maybe we can find out where Mr. Woller lived, and this Mr. Ullman and the others. Maybe they left clues. We could start with Mr. Woller. We already know what he looks like." Boo began to copy Cisco's lists onto Grandma's shopping-list tablet.

"We do?" Poppy was surprised.

Boo looked pleased with herself. "Sure. I asked the reception-desk lady and one of the other-desk ladies at the savings and loan company. They remembered him because of his shaggy white eyebrows and funny little—what're they called, those silly chin beards?"

"Goatees," said Grandma.

Boo nodded. "That's it. A goatee, like that old guy who was in the TV fried-chicken commercials when I was little."

Grandma perked up suddenly. "He was old? Oh, my! Do you suppose—"

Boo and Cisco and Poppy chimed, "*What?*" all three at once.

Grandma's blue eyes were as bright as Babba's.

"Well, if he's old enough, these crooks could be the same bunch as the old storm-window swindlers. Couldn't they? Why, they could even be the Rufus Roofing Company gang. That was only twenty years or so ago."

Cisco leaned forward excitedly, but Boo was doubt-ful.

"Why would they keep coming back?" she asked. "It would be too dangerous, wouldn't it?"

"Because of the easy pickings, that's why," Grandma said sagely. "And what danger? Nobody can identify 'em. If they wait eight or ten years before they come back, the last batch of old folks they robbed will be dead and gone, and a new batch ready and waiting."

" 'Cept this time it was the loan companies that saw them, Grandma, not old folks," piped up Poppy.

Grandma wasn't fazed. "Maybe they don't plan to come back again. Maybe they're retiring. I think, my dears, that we ought to round up descriptions of every 'new owner' on Cisco's list. Boo, you can help with the phoning. Then, Cisco, you and Poppy can go to the library to check out the old newspaper articles about the storm-window swindlers. Who knows? Maybe some of the descriptions will match up. Then we really would have something to tell the police."

Cisco gave a sigh. More legwork. Grandma's plan sounded as if it were straight out of chapter 9, "Follow Up on Your Hunches," in *The Young Detective's Handbook*. He ought to be excited, but where was the fun in collecting clues if your hunch was that all of the villains had left town? Where were the shivers? How could you be Sherlock Holmes or Lieutenant Columbo or Charlie Chan without villains and danger?

All you could be was Cisco Smith, whose house was being—no, already had been—stolen.

Cisco shivered.

MR. SMITH DID A BIT OF DETECTIVE WORK HIMSELF. ON HIS lunch hour he called the police department downtown to ask what police station he should call to speak to Officer Art Delatorre. Mr. Smith and Art Delatorre had gone from first grade through high school together, and Mr. Smith remembered hearing that his old classmate had joined the police force.

It turned out that he was now Lieutenant Delatorre, a detective, and working at the downtown headquarters. Mr. Smith's call was transferred to Lieutenant Delatorre, and he found himself making an appointment to meet him downtown at four o'clock.

By the time Mr. Smith reached the City-County Building and found Elvira a parking place, he was almost late. Art Delatorre came to the main desk to meet him. After a detour by way of the coffee machine, he steered Mr. Smith to an empty interview room.

"Look here, Dan." The lieutenant leaned forward in his chair when he had heard Mr. Smith's story. "It may not turn out to be any help, but I've heard all this before. Three times, in fact. All of them this year. I'd swear something fishy was going on, but we couldn't get a handle on it."

Mr. Smith sat up. "Then there *is* a police investigation?"

"No. If the court says a grant deed is legal, we're pretty much out of it. No crime, no crime busters. We did send out tracers on the guys who are supposed to have bought the houses from the old dears, but didn't turn up a thing. And disappearing's not illegal, so for us that's pretty much it."

Mr. Smith finished off his coffee. " 'For you'? What does that mean?"

Lieutenant Delatorre shrugged. "You could take Keystone Savings and Loan to civil court and try to prove the deed's a forgery. That takes money, though. Lawyers. Handwriting experts. A doctor to say your mom still has all her marbles. None of the others could afford that. Can you?"

Mr. Smith shook his head. "No way. Look, what I don't get is how these guys can get away with registering fake deeds."

"Neither could I until I phoned the recorder's office. All you need to register a new grant deed is to have the seller's signature witnessed by a notary public. The recorder's office doesn't run any checks. All your house thief has to worry about is finding a crooked notary."

"You mean there's nothing to stop people like Mom

and the others getting ripped off? Even when they haven't signed anything? The thieves could file forged deeds and no one would even *check*?"

The lieutenant nodded.

Mr. Smith stood with a sigh. "The whole thing's crazy."

Lieutenant Delatorre was thoughtful. "Tell you what, Danny. I'll take a look at those deeds myself on the off chance the court missed something. I'll let you know."

Mr. Smith gave him a tired grin. "You do that. I'm going home and take a nap. This house mess really gets me down."

Out in the garden shed that stood half in Grandma's backyard and half in Mrs. Finnerty's, Babba put the last touches on Cookie's new bed. The bed was an old-fashioned laundry basket with a broken rim. Its mattress was a gunnysack stuffed with dried grass and covered with a threadbare old towel. Babba didn't know how many kittens cats could have at one time, but the basket was large enough for Cookie and at least a dozen small Cookies. A whole basketful would be nice.

The new bed sat in the far corner, next to Mr. Havlichek's worktable. Grandma had said, "No cat," but Babba had taken care of that. The bed was on the Finnerty side of the shed. Beside it stood the old dog bowl with TOBY lettered on its side and a cracked yellow cereal bowl Mr. Havlichek had rescued from

Mrs. Finnerty's trash can. One was for water, the other for cat food. On the wall above the bed, Babba had fastened a picture of a basketful of fluffy white kittens. She had cut the picture out of one of Grandma's old magazines and stuck it up with a large gob of Cisco's blue stickum. Cookie's new home was ready.

It was time to go find Cookie and the kittens.

Babba had planned every step. It would be at least an hour before Grandma called everyone to supper. Babba stood up, brushed off her dusty knees, and crossed the shed to pick up the basket Grandma used when she picked beans or squash or tomatoes from her garden.

Then she went into the garden and pulled up the only lettuce she could find and took it in to Grandma.

Grandma was in the kitchen, snapping green beans into short pieces into a bowl in her lap. The meat loaf that had sat in its pan on the table, with two strips of bacon down its back, was already in the oven. Nine fat potatoes and a just-baked pie stood in its place.

Babba showed the lettuce to Grandma. It was the tough, stiff-leaved kind, but the heat had left it limp and draggled.

"Dear me, the poor thing looks more like a dust rag than a lettuce, doesn't it?" asked Grandma. "Maybe a good soaking will perk it up. Close the plug in the sink and run some water, will you, punkin? Then you can take the basket back out to the shed, if you like."

"Where's Daddy? And everybody?" Babba asked. She dragged the kitchen step stool to the sink to make herself tall enough to reach the plug.

Grandma finished the beans and picked up her paring knife and a potato.

"Your daddy's taking a nap on the living-room sofa. He got back from the downtown police station just a bit ago. Boo is on the telephone. Cisco isn't back from the library, and Poppy's upstairs tweezing Danny's prickles out."

Earlier Danny, intent on earning more pennies for weeding, had waded through the berry brambles and finished up by picking a tall and very prickly giant thistle. His yelp of pain had grown to a bellow that brought everyone in both houses—and even a young man from the house beyond Mrs. Finnerty's—at a run.

"Good," said Babba.

Without hurrying, she turned off the water and put the lettuce in the sink to soak. Then she returned the step stool to its place, picked up the basket and, with a sweet smile for Grandma, headed for the back porch.

At the foot of the porch steps, she made a quick left turn. Under cover of the spirea bushes, she darted around the corner of the house and headed for the street.

The parking space in front of Mrs. Tuttlebee's house was empty. That meant Mr. Zimmerman, the Wicked

Witch's roomer, had not come home yet. Babba stood at the corner of the barberry hedge and thought. The Witch was probably cooking dinner. The kitchen was probably at the back of the house. Kitchens usually were. That still left Poppy's mysterious man who came to the window.

Rumpelstiltskin.

Babba shivered. What if Rumpelstiltskin looked out and spied her as she slipped through the front gate? And if she tried to push her way through the prickly hedge, he might hear the rustling and look out and see the bushes moving. Besides, if she went through the hedge, she would get all scratched up and Grandma would make Boo or Poppy paint the scratches with Merthiolate. Babba hated Merthiolate. The Merthiolate stain on her old shorts was still there after dozens of washings.

Babba walked to the front gate and, with the basket hung over one arm, used both hands to open the gate, pushing down on it as she pulled. The gate groaned instead of squeaking. She closed it just as carefully, then calmly cut across the little patch of lawn and around the corner of the front porch. In the deep shade past the corner of the house she saw Poppy's trash cans and, ten or twelve yards further along, the stairs up to Nancy Wheat's apartment.

Picking her way carefully along the path between the piles of junk, Babba searched along the fence. She looked for the hole she had watched through when she saw Rumpelstiltskin and heard the kitten's *mew*.

She did not find it until she was almost past the side porch Poppy had described. Poppy had said that Cookie and her fish had come out the porch door and disappeared. That meant her hiding place must be somewhere between the porch and the front corner of the house. Babba peered behind the stacks of firewood, tugged at the rusty padlock fastening the doors to an unused outdoor cellar stairway, and pushed at grimy cellar windows set in the thick foundation wall.

The third window swung inward at first touch.

Babba set down the basket, dropped to her knees, pushed the window inward, up and away from her—it was hinged at the top—and squinted into the darkness.

"Cookie?" she called softly. "Kitty-kitty?"

There was an odd little noise, halfway between a rustle and a clatter, but no cat or kitten sounds.

Babba looked around for a stick to wedge the window open and spied a broken broomstick behind the trash cans. With the window propped up so that it would not swing down and bang her on the head, she stuck her head and shoulders in for a better look. The cellar room *had* to be Cookie's hiding place.

If it was, it was a strange one. From about a foot below the window a high heap of chunky, dusty black rocks sloped away into the darkness. Babba was puzzled. Why would anyone keep rocks in the basement? With one hand grasping the windowsill, she leaned forward to pick up one of the small rocks. Teetering, she heard the small, thin cry she had heard before.

Mew!

Babba's head went up. Losing her balance, she tipped through the window and fell head over heels, tumbling down the black rocky heap with the basket and bit of broomstick rolling after.

13

THE CELLAR WAS DARK, BUT IT WAS COOL, TOO. BABBA DID not like the dark much even when she was safe in bed, but the cool air was welcome after the heavy, sticky heat outdoors.

A little light did fall through the window from the shadowy passage along the side of the house. It showed the glittery black track she had plowed down the heap of stones under the window, but it was not strong enough to reach into the corners of the little room. A bare light bulb hung overhead, but its string was so short that not even Boo could have reached it. Babba shivered as she picked herself up. In a witch's house, dark corners might mean mice or rats or spiders— even if the witch wasn't *really* a witch.

Spiders! Babba brushed quickly at her shirt and shorts and then her arms and legs. Instead of creepy-crawlies, she felt a gritty dust that stuck fast or smeared wherever her skin was damp from the heat. As her eyes became accustomed to the darkness, she saw black dust and ugly smears on her arms and legs and shorts and T-shirt. She began to sniffle. The kittens were quite forgotten. All she wanted was Grandma's bathtub, with lots of soapy water in it.

The heap of stones did not look very steep, but when Babba tried to climb it, she only slithered down again. When she stopped sliding, she found herself up to her ankles in the strange black stones. The second time, she backed up a step or two and tried to run up the heap. The effort took her almost halfway up, but then she slid slowly back down again, sinking in halfway to her knees.

As Babba struggled free of the heap, she fell again. When she stood, grit filled her sandals and even in between her toes. She was indignant. People shouldn't *have* windows where she could fall through them. If they had them, they ought to have chairs or boxes handy for climbing out again. They *certainly* shouldn't keep piles of dirty rocks in their cellars. She bent to pick up the basket that had tumbled through the window with her.

Mew.

Babba straightened. The sound was tiny, but so clear that she knew it came from nearby.

The little room's walls were built of stone, and thick. Squinting in the shadowy darkness, she spied a door that stood midway between two of the dark corners. It was open only a crack, but that was enough for Babba to squirm her fingers through and pull.

"Kitty-kitty?" she whispered.

The room beyond was lit dimly through two high windows and a ventilation grate at the base of the wall opposite. A gleaming new oil-fired furnace stood midway along the window wall. In the far corner squatted the huge, domed hulk of an old coal furnace. Fat vent pipes had fed its heat into a system of ducts that carried it throughout the house above, but they had been dismantled. A few pieces of the old vent pipe were stacked in another corner. Pennsylvania furnaces were nothing like the upstairs gas-fired furnaces in many Los Angeles houses. Babba knew the old iron hulk was a furnace even though she did not know it burned coal instead of gas or oil. Grandma Smith had one like it, only hers was not so rusty. Babba had explored Grandma's basement with Cisco. Cisco had once seen a furnace like it in a creepy old movie on TV.

"Cookie? Pretty kitty?" Babba whispered.

Meow.

The door at the bottom of the old furnace—where ashes once were raked out—had broken off its hinges. Inside, something moved. Babba hesitated. Then she decided that kneeling down couldn't make her knees much dirtier. So she did.

"Oh!"

Cookie had dragged an old gunnysack in on top of the long-dead ashes. She lay on it with five small kittens. Their eyes were still not open.

107

"Oooooh!" Babba sighed greedily, her own eyes shining.

"Hat-CHOO! Dratted cats!" roared a voice behind her.

14

CISCO AND LEE CHIANG WENT OFF TO THE CARNEGIE LI-
brary together. Lee thought finding out about the old
swindle was a great idea. Great-Aunt Chiang agreed
that the possibility the house thefts and the old storm-
window swindle might be connected was well worth
investigating. Lee had not finished restocking the
shelves and there was still the floor to mop, but his
mother, bringing baby Lily in a basket cradle, came
downstairs to the market to take his place.

"I thought your sister Poppy was coming," Lee said
as the two boys headed for the door.

Cisco shrugged. "Grandma showed us the library
on a map and Poppy said it was too far to go when it
was so hot out."

"Then I should return these to Mr. Fazio," Lee said
as he opened the Top Luck Market's screen door. He
lifted the worn leather binoculars case that hung on a
braided cord around his neck and grinned. "I was
going to show Poppy strange Mrs. Tuttlebee's strange
house from a good, safe distance."

"From over across the park? Hey, you can show me. Besides, Poppy's already seen it. She's been *in* it." Cisco described Poppy's visit to Tottering Towers to Lee as they walked up Harkness Street toward Forbes Avenue.

The University of Pittsburgh's law school, where Peter Quilty and Nancy Wheat were students, turned out to be a biggish building only a short distance along Forbes Avenue from the corner of Harkness Street. As the boys passed it and the university's Hillman Library, Cisco gawked at a skyscraper of a tower across the avenue, not far ahead. It soared skyward from the middle of a grassy, tree-clad park the size of five or six city blocks.

"What's *that*?"

"The Cathedral of Learning," Lee said. "My father says there is nothing like it in the world. Uncle Yao-Lung—Uncle Joe—took me to see it. It is full of class-rooms, and many are very beautiful. There is even one decorated Chinese-style."

The boys crossed a wide parking lot to the welcome shade of the two rows of sycamore trees along the far side. Once beyond the trees, Cisco found himself facing one side of a large, handsome old building. The sign at the entrance read CARNEGIE LIBRARY.

"Wow! It must be the biggest library in the *world*."

"No, only this side and along the back are the library," Lee explained. "The front corner is a concert hall, and beyond it is the Museum of Natural History. With dinosaurs."

"Real ones? Ones built out of real bones, I mean?"

Lee nodded.

Cisco walked faster. The danger that Grandma Smith might lose her house had been frightening from the first. Now it began to look as if having to move away and lose the neighborhood would be terrible, too.

The boys asked directions of a guard in the library's entrance hall. Newspapers, he said, were to be found in the Periodicals Room. "Upstairs. Turn right, and down at the end of the hall, turn left down the hallway across from the Pennsylvania Room. Can't miss it."

Cisco half expected to find a big room with tall shelves stacked high with newspapers. Instead, the Periodicals Room seemed to have only a rack, where the Pittsburgh paper and the latest New York and Washington and Philadelphia papers hung, waiting for readers. The librarian at the desk at the entrance explained that the back copies were all photographed and stored on microfilm, which took up much less space. To read the microfilm, the boys would have to use a machine called a microfilm reader. She nodded toward the area on the right of the entrance, where four rows of the machines huddled atop their reading tables. From the side the machines and the readers using them looked almost like short, stumpy video-arcade games with players glued to the screens.

"Are kids allowed to use them?" Cisco asked doubtfully.

The librarian folded her arms and studied the boys from head to toe as if she were trying to guess their shirt and shoe sizes. Then she smiled.

"I think we can risk it. I'll thread the film into the machine. That's the only tricky part. What paper do you need to see, and what date?"

Cisco frowned. "It was eight or nine years ago, my grandma and her friend say. There was this reporter lady who wrote an article about some crooks who went around selling storm windows to old people."

The librarian's eyebrows shot up. "You want to read through two whole years' worth of papers? You'd be cross-eyed before you reached the first Fourth of July. A year of the *Post-Gazette* could be twelve whole rolls, and the *Pittsburgh Press* double that. Even if you each took a year, you'd probably be here for the next two days. You wouldn't happen to know the reporter's name, would you?"

Cisco frowned. "Grandma met her, but she can't remember for sure. She says the reporter's last name was kind of like her own first name. Her name's Alice."

The librarian shook her head as she ran a finger down a list of telephone numbers taped to the desk and then picked up the phone. "It's not much to go on, but I can try the *Press*'s research department." She tapped out the number on the phone.

The boys listened eagerly as she asked the newspaper's research-department clerk if his computer knew whether eight or nine years ago there had been a woman crime or feature writer on the paper's staff with a name something like Alice.

"No, not Alice. A last name something *like* Alice. Allison, maybe. . . . McAllister? Could be. . . . Cass McAllister. . . . Yes, it's worth a try. We're looking for a story about property swindles in Oakland."

She covered the receiver with her hand. "He's looking up Ms. McAllister's stories from back then." She waited for several moments and then grinned. "Bingo! That has to be it. What's the date and page number?"

She jotted numbers on a piece of scrap paper, thanked the research clerk, hung up, and went to an aisle nearby where she pulled out a shallow storage drawer, ran a finger down the rows of small boxes, and chose one. Beckoning the boys to follow, she led them to an unused microfilm reader. There the boys watched closely as she took out the spool of film and threaded it into the machine. Switching on the power, she ran through several weeks of newspaper pages on fast forward. Then she slowed, scanning the page numbers, until she came to an article titled SCAM ARTISTS TARGET OAKLAND SENIORS.

"There you are. I hope it's what you're looking for."
It was.

The boys crowded onto the chair in front of the microfilm reader so that they both could read the image projected onto the machine's screen.

"What is a 'scam artist'?" Lee asked with a puzzled frown.

"Same as a swindler. A con man," Cisco answered absentmindedly. He skimmed through the first paragraphs of the article. "Hey, look at this!" He pointed excitedly to the last part of the second paragraph.

> This latest rash of complaints from Oakland residents reveals a vicious new twist to one of the oldest of household swindles, the storm-window scam.
>
> Usually the scam is simple. Homeowners are approached by high-pressure door-to-door salesmen who convince them that the cost of the windows will be offset by the savings in heating bills. A contract is signed. The salesman then obtains a down payment of from one to two thousand dollars. Once the money is in his pocket, he disappears and is not heard from again.
>
> The new version takes advantage of the fact that many elderly people who cannot afford large down payments nevertheless own their homes free and clear.

"Like Grandma and Mr. Fazio," Cisco said. He pointed again.

> . . . No down payment is required. Instead, when the contract is signed, the sample copy—the one customers are encouraged to read, small print and all—is a straightforward agreement to purchase storm windows. The salesman's copies appear to be the same,

but are in fact sale contracts for unsuspecting "customers' " homes.

In mid-September five Oakland home owners ordered storm windows from a still-unidentified salesman. In the middle of October all five home owners received eviction notices. In rapid succession titles to the properties had been transferred to five new owners: Albert Bakkus, Charles Dennison, Eugene Fossick, George Hallinan, and Ian Jeffries. Bakkus and the others had sold all five houses at auction, pocketed cashiers' checks totaling $314,000, and vanished. At court hearings last week all five "sales" were ruled valid because "the signatures on the grant deeds appear to be genuine and the present purchasers bought the houses in good faith." None of the original owners could afford legal representation. All five lost their homes.

Cisco looked up, indignant. "It's different, but it's the same. I bet you it *is* the same guys!"

"Shh!" Lee looked around and met several older readers' stares.

"Okay," Cisco whispered, "but it *is*. And look down here. It's got descriptions of the crooks, too." He dug in his pocket for his notebook and pencil.

Lee was already several paragraphs ahead. "Here she tells about another scheme, twenty years ago. But it was very different—a roofing company that did nothing but paint some of the roofs with tar."

Cisco nodded as he wrote. "Rufus Roofing. Mr. Havlichek told us about that."

Lee smothered a giggle. "It says Mrs. Tuttlebee

115

called Mr. Rufus a 'stringy, sour-tempered scoundrel.' She said that she should have known he was up to no good, because when he rented a room in her house he kept the room too neat and his suitcases locked. She must have tried to snoop."

Cisco wrote *Stringy + Sour.*

When Cisco had finished taking notes, the boys rewound the spool of film and put it back into its box. Returning it to the librarian, they made their way downstairs and out into the sticky afternoon heat.

"I don't get it." Cisco frowned. "The Wicked Witch said he was stringy. That means tall, doesn't it? But Mrs. Finnerty called him 'little.' "

Lee shrugged. "Perhaps Mrs. Finnerty does not remember clearly. It has been a long time. And the article was written ten years after Mr. Rufus disappeared. Perhaps Mrs. Tuttlebee exaggerated to make her story more interesting."

"Maybe," Cisco admitted.

Lee looked at his watch. "It's five o'clock. What time in the evening do you eat at your house?"

Cisco made a face. "At six. When the "Star Trek" reruns are on TV. Back home they were on at seven. I can't even watch the ending after we finish dinner, because my dad watches the news then. Why?"

"Because," Lee said, "that means we still have time for me to show you Mrs. Tuttlebee's house. It looks even odder from this side of the hollow than it does from your street."

116

It was still too hot for running, but Lee led the way at a fast walk to a road that angled past the rear of the library and into a park. The name on the sign read SCHENLEY PARK. After a short distance the ground fell away steeply, like the hillside at the end of Grandma Smith's street. The road became a bridge across the street and railway line that ran down the hollow below. Cisco's knees felt a little wobbly when he looked over the edge, but he followed Lee along the walkway to the middle of the bridge. Lee stopped there and pointed across the hollow.

"See? Over there. It is the grayish one with turrets." Lee opened the binoculars case and took out Mr. Fazio's field glasses. He handed them to Cisco.

Cisco, his eyes on the little cluster of turrets that reared out of the trees along the rim of the hollow, put the braided leather cord around his neck and raised the heavy binoculars. The house opposite sprang at him like a great, glassy-eyed gray spider.

"Wow!" Cisco almost jumped back a step.

"They are very good glasses," Lee said. "Very strong. When Uncle Joe and I went to our first Pirates baseball game, Mr. Fazio let us take them. They were for bird-watching, but he has not used them since Mrs. Fazio died."

The house was larger than Cisco had expected. From the front it had looked no bigger than his grandmother's, but the side view showed that from front to back it was much longer. Two narrow balcony porches like the two halves of a turret were stuck onto the

117

side of the house and added to its crazy-castle look. Through the trees he could make out the crisscrosses of window panes along the basement level. He moved the glasses to the right, toward the trees below the fence at the end of Hillyard Street.

"Hey, there's a tree house just below the end of our street, and—" He stopped abruptly and turned the glasses back toward Mrs. Tuttlebee's house.

"What is it?" Lee demanded. "What do you see?"

"I dunno," he said. "It *can't* be." Frowning, he lowered the field glasses, then raised them for another look.

"Cannot be *what*?" Lee demanded. He reached out to snatch at the binoculars, but caught himself and jammed his hands into his pockets.

Cisco peered at each of the patches of basement window panes that showed through the trees. The panes seemed to be part of a large picture window. But—nothing.

The small, blurry Babba-like figure he thought he had seen peering out, hands up and pressed against the glass, was gone.

15

"HAT-*CHOO!*"

Babba whirled so fast that she lost her balance and sat down on the dusty furnace-room floor with a *plop.* But no one was there.

The sneezer sneezed again. "Hat-*CHOO!*"

The sound was loud, but a little muffled. It sounded as if it might have come from behind a not-quite-closed door. Yet except for the door through which Babba herself had come, the doors into the furnace room were closed. One, between the two filthy high-up windows, must once have led to the outdoor cellar stairs, but now it was boarded shut. Another, to the left of the new furnace, was closed, too.

The sneezer's voice growled loudly. "Dratted cats! I'll sure be glad to be shut of the whole hairy crew of you. C'mon, you, get out of my road."

Babba heard a cat's sharp yowl and a familiar *rattle-clash*, the sound of curtain rings on a rod. With it came a sudden wash of light through the grate at the bottom of the inner wall opposite the windows.

Once upon a time the grating in the thick wall must have been a hot-air outlet connected to the old furnace. Now, as Babba discovered when she squatted to peer through it, it made a fine window into the room next door.

The room wasn't at all like a basement room. It wasn't even like any upstairs room Babba had ever seen. Most of the far wall was a long row of floor-length French windows that looked out into the hillside trees. Babba's peephole was placed so that she could see only the middle and one end of the long room, but because of the windows, that part was as bright as if it were a stage and Babba the audience sitting in the dark. She thought it the most wonderful room in the world.

There were cats everywhere. The fattest and furriest cats Babba had ever seen were curled up on the sofa and chairs, stretched out along the sofa back, draped over the tables, and even—two of them—shut up in the large bird cages that stood on the tables at each end of the sofa. There were ginger-colored cats, black ones with white faces and paws, white ones, calico ones, white ones with black spots, brown-and-black ones, and gray ones. Babba tried to count them, but had to stop at twenty because it was the highest number she knew.

Strangely, every one of the cats was as quiet as if it were a stuffed toy. Only the twitching tails and a yawn or two showed that they weren't. And every one that Babba could see, even the ones that pretended to be asleep, watched the man.

The man who had sneezed was Mr. Zimmerman, the

Wicked Witch's roomer. Babba had seen him after breakfast, dusting off his shiny car before he drove away. Somehow he made her think of Rumpelstiltskin, the little man she had seen dancing around the bonfire in the backyard. But that was silly. They weren't at all alike. Rumpelstiltskin had been bald on top, with a shaggy fringe of mousy brown hair. He had had a pointy nose and knobbly knees and wore funny high-tops and shorts with fancy suspenders. Maybe he hadn't really had the wooden leg, but a wooden leg did make the story better.

Babba had not seen Mr. Zimmerman up close before. He had sleek black hair, a thin little mustache, and a bulbous nose, and every time he sneezed he gave a little hop. "Hat-*CHOO!*" Hop. He wore a suit, as if he were going to church, and while he knotted his tie, he made silly faces at himself in a mirror on the wall behind the sofa.

"Hat-*CHOO!*" Hop!

Once his tie was tied, the man opened the French door at the right end of the window wall and went out, locking it behind him.

When he did not come back, Babba opened the furnace-room door and tiptoed in. She crossed to the windows and stood, nose and hands against the panes of glass, looking out through the treetops. Then she turned back to the cats.

Lee leaned out over the bridge's railing. "What do you see now?" he asked.

121

Cisco answered slowly. "A man, I think. On a path down the hill." After the first brief glimpse, all he could see through the gaps in the trees were flickers of movement. The flickers traveled steadily downward toward the retaining wall that ran along the steep foot of the hill.

"Where did he come from?" asked Lee.

"I dunno." Cisco's wrists were growing tired from the heavy binoculars, but he held them steady.

It really was a man. In a gray business suit. He appeared suddenly in a cleared area above a gap in the wall. Through that gap a short stub of a lane, only long enough for two parked cars, angled upward. The man made his way down to a dark-colored car. A moment later he drove out to the road, turned left, left again at the next corner, and was gone.

Cisco lowered the binoculars and blinked.

"What did you see?" Lee demanded eagerly.

"It was—at least, I *think* it was—Mrs. Tuttlebee's roomer. I saw him when he came home from work yesterday. I think he just came down from her house and got into his car to drive *back* to her house."

The two boys looked at each other.

Cisco nodded solemnly. "I say we stake out the Wicked Witch's house."

"Yes indeed. But tomorrow, not now." Lee made a sour face. "Now I must go back to the market."

Boo hung up the telephone receiver and scowled at her last entry on the list of house thieves. *Oscar Pen-*

nyman—medium tall, white hair + mustache, blue eyes, beaky nose. Uses a cane. Wishing wouldn't make it any better; none of the descriptions matched. All five were as different as—as giraffes and hippos. Well, almost. So why did she still have a niggly feeling that somehow they were alike?

Boo headed back along the hall toward the kitchen, where Grandma was peeling boiled potatoes for potato salad. Grandma looked up.

"Did you finally get hold of the loan officer at Iron City Savings who saw Florrie Gallo's Mr. Pennyman?"

"Yes, just now. She was working late. But Mr. Pennyman doesn't sound like any of the others." Boo reread the list once more. The niggly feeling was still there, but—No. Nothing. She sighed.

"Maybe when Cisco gets back we'll find out what the storm-window salesmen looked like," she said. "Maybe *they*'ll match somebody. What did that Mr. Rufus, the roof man, look like, Grandma?"

"It's been a long time." Grandma closed her eyes and thought. "Let's see: I remember he had red hair, with long sideburns. Rusty red, not carroty. I never saw him really close to, but he didn't strike me as being tall. Oh, and he had what we called a 'thermometer nose' when I was a child. It was long and thin, with a little ball on the end, you see."

Boo sat down at the kitchen table and added Mr. Rufus to her list. "What about his eyes?" she asked.

Grandma shook her head as she sliced and then

diced the potatoes. "I never saw 'em. He always wore sunglasses. I—Goodness gracious!"

Poppy had appeared in the doorway with Danny in tow. She had been very generous with the Merthiolate when she painted his thistle welts and bramble scratches. His arms and legs were crisscrossed with bright orangey red streaks, and Poppy had turned several of them into doodles. Danny had a tulip growing up one leg, a daisy on one knee, and a bee on his wrist.

"Look, Gran'ma! I got dattoos!"

"So I see," said Grandma dryly. "Very nice. Do I have any Merthiolate left?"

Poppy flushed. "Only a little bit," she admitted in a small voice.

"Ah, well, good enough. Poppy, you and Babba can set the table for supper. We'll each need an extra fork, for dessert. I made a pie. Lemon meringue."

"Lemonarang! Lemonarang!" cheered Danny.

Boo looked around. "Where *is* Babba?"

"Out back," Grandma said. "Probably in the garden shed. My guess is the child's making a nest for that moth-eaten excuse for a cat. She's been as sweet as two sugar pies all afternoon."

"Then she *is* up to something," Boo agreed.

Poppy crossed to the screen door to call. "Babba! Come help set the table."

When there was no answer, Boo got up and went to the door. "*Bab*ba!" she shouted.

Grandma stood and held on to the sink with one

hand as she opened the refrigerator door. "Goodness! No need to bellow like a bull calf. It won't hurt one of you to go out and fetch her."

Boo went, but Babba wasn't in the garden shed or either garden. Mr. Havlichek, who was sitting in a lawn chair under the apple tree next door, said he hadn't seen her for a good half hour or more.

In the kitchen, Grandma had already finished beating together the eggs and olive oil for homemade mayonnaise. "Not there? She must be upstairs, then. Poppy dear, you run up and find her. The rest of us will get out of this hot kitchen until the meat loaf is ready to come out of the oven. At least tomorrow we won't have to cook. We'll have meat loaf enough for two meals."

When Poppy came down again from upstairs, the others were in the living room.

"She's not up there," Poppy announced. "Not anywhere."

"Who's not?" Mr. Smith, awakening from his nap, sat up on the sofa, rubbed his eyes, and stretched.

"It's Babba," Grandma said. "The last I saw of her she went out back, but that was at least half an hour ago. I wager she's gone chasing after that ratty little cat again."

"Count on it," Mr. Smith said. He smothered a yawn and pushed himself to his feet. "Babba has a one-track mind and enough nerve for a rhinoceros."

"I'll go ask everybody at Mrs. Finnerty's," Boo offered.

"I—I think the cat came from down at Mrs. Tuttlebee's," Poppy said nervously.

"Just what we need," her father said grimly. "A run-in with Terrible Tilly. That'll be the icing on my day. Where's Cisco? We'll need him if we're going to cover the neighborhood."

"Not back from the library yet," Boo called as she banged out the front screen door.

Mr. Smith looked at his watch. "A quarter of six. Good gravy, he must be coming by way of Philadelphia."

Cisco was up a tree. After leaving Lee behind at the market, he had made his way back toward Grandma's. Then, at the corner of Hillyard Street, he remembered the tree house. The clock at the Top Luck Market had said five thirty-five, so there was time for a quick look before supper at six.

Hillyard Street came to a dead end several yards beyond Mrs. Tuttlebee's front gate, where her roomer's shiny black Buick was—no surprise—now parked. Short lengths of old telephone pole, neatly whitewashed, had been set upright in concrete, two feet or so apart, to make a barrier between the foot of the street and the hillside below. A fat steel cable threaded through holes drilled in the posts served as guardrail. On Mrs. Tuttlebee's side, the barberry hedge reached out prickly arms to bar the way past the barrier. On the other side, her neighbor across the street had planted geraniums and daisies. Half a dozen crooked steps, made from pieces of broken concrete sidewalk, led down through the daisies into knee-high grass and weeds. Below the grass and weeds came a few scrubby shrubs, and then the trees. Cisco took his notebook from the hip pocket of his shorts, shoved it into a front pocket as deep as it would go, and started down.

The tree-house tree, a large maple, stood only a short way down into the woods. Strips of wood had been nailed crosswise up the lower trunk for footholds, but these were old and rotten. The bottom one splintered when Cisco tested his weight on it. He pulled off the others and used a stone to break off or flatten the rusty nails. Swarming up a tree trunk might not be as easy on a hillside as on level ground, but Cisco was an old hand at tree climbing. On the second try he pulled himself up into the crotch of the tree. From there on, it was easy going.

The tree house was high up, perched on a platform supported by three stout branches and the main trunk. It would be perfect for Tarzan or Indiana Jones games. Cisco hugged the trunk in delight.

The platform, he decided, must have been built by someone's father, because its framework was made of heavy lumber bolted together. It had tilted a bit as the tree grew, but was still in one piece and looked safely solid. What was left of the walls and roof was flimsier.

Cisco didn't trust them. He was careful not to touch them as he climbed up and in.

The view of Tottering Towers, off to the left, was mostly screened by the leafy branches. Through one opening Cisco could see much of the wide wall of French windows on the basement level, but nothing of the room behind its panes. He kicked away a drift of old leaves and sat down on the platform to watch. Only five minutes, he promised himself.

The trouble was, by sitting down he lost his view of the windows. Instead, looking through another gap in the leaves, he found himself with a front-row-center seat on Hillyard Street just as Boo dashed out of Grandma's front door. To his surprise, she cut across the grass and jumped over the low picket fence between the two houses to get to Mrs. Finnerty's front porch. When his father appeared on Grandma's front porch to shout "Babba! Babba! Where in blazes are you?" Cisco sat up in alarm. What was up?

It had to be more than everyday Babba mischief. Mrs. Finnerty, Mr. Havlichek, and Peter Quilty came out on their porch with Boo. Grandma, Poppy, and Danny joined Mr. Smith. Cisco could hear the excited voices, but not what anyone was saying. It was like watching TV with the sound turned down. Then, suddenly, everyone except for Grandma and Danny was going in a different direction, up or down or across the street. They called Babba's name, went to neighbors' doors, knocked, and waved their hands and talked.

Poppy came running down the sidewalk straight toward him. She stopped in front of Mrs. Tuttlebee's front gate, then took a deep breath and let herself in. Cisco blinked, but then he remembered Nancy Wheat. Poppy must be headed for Nancy's attic room.

It was all very puzzling. Babba, lost? Mr. Smith always said Babba's head was screwed on more firmly than any other head in the family. She always knew exactly what she was doing, and usually got exactly what she set her mind on. She must have gone after her silly old cat—what else? And if Poppy was right about where the cat lived, there was only one place Babba could have gone.

Just then Poppy reappeared with Nancy and climbed the steps of Mrs. Tuttlebee's front porch. Surveillance forgotten, Cisco scrambled to his feet and headed for the tree-house doorway. Watching a show wasn't half as much fun as being in it.

16

"SHE'S REALLY ANGRY," NANCY WHEAT SAID AFTER MRS. Tuttlebee slammed the door. Waiting with Poppy on the rickety front porch, Nancy was a picture of gloom. "I hope she doesn't raise my rent to get even."

"Anyhow, she's *looking*," Poppy said nervously. She jiggled up and down on the balls of her feet.

Both Poppy and Nancy jumped at the sound of the gate behind them clanging shut.

"Cisco! Guess what!"

Halfway through Poppy's account of Babba's disappearance, Nancy gave one of Poppy's braids a warning tug. "Keep it for later, kids," she whispered. "She's coming back."

A key scraped in the front-door lock. The door creaked open and Mrs. Tuttlebee's sharp nose and sharper black eyes appeared above the safety chain.

"Who're you?" she snapped at Cisco. "Oh, another snooping Smith. Hmph! The answer's the same whether there's two or a dozen of you. I don't have any blacky-brown cat. Or any kittens. My cat's gray-and-white and stays indoors. *And* there's no child in my house. I've looked, and that's that. So clear out and make pests of yourselves somewhere else."

Poppy found enough courage to edge out from behind Nancy.

"Please, missus. You didn't look very long. Babba's a *very* good hider."

"Is that so, Miss Sassy?" The old lady gave her a lemon-sour look. "Well, I happen to be a *very* good looker, and what I want is for you Smiths to take yourselves off my property. Miss Wheat, you make sure they go."

She slammed the door with a loud bang. The children heard her footsteps patter away.

Nancy, scowling, jammed her hands into her jeans pockets. "Old bat!"

"Knock again," Cisco urged. "She doesn't understand. She couldn't have looked hard enough. She doesn't know Babba. Babba once hid in a wastebasket."

"And once in the clothes in the clothes drier," Poppy said excitedly. "It was *awful*, because Momma didn't know, and she turned it on. Babba almost got dried to death. It burned some of her curls off."

"Honest." Cisco nodded. "And a big button burned her leg. You can still see the mark."

"Sorry, kids." Nancy gave an uncomfortable shrug. "The old grouch isn't budgeable, and I can't afford to get her mad at me. You heard what she said about the mother cat. It isn't hers. Come on, let's go find your dad."

"I don't believe her, Daddy." Cisco was stubborn. "What if she's holding Babba prisoner?"

"That's goofy," Boo declared. "Why would she?"

Mr. Smith's eyebrows drew together into a scowl. "Cisco, this is serious."

Poppy spoke up quickly. "She might want to scare Babba so she wouldn't come snooping anymore."

Mr. Smith raised his eyebrows, but Nancy nodded.

"You know, she just might. She's pretty nutty."

Mr. Smith ran a nervous hand through his hair as he considered. Mrs. Tuttlebee had always been odd, even when he was a small boy. He looked at his watch. Six-twenty.

"It's light until nine, but if we don't find Babba in the next fifteen minutes, I'm going to phone the police. We can let them deal with Mrs. Tuttlebee. I can't. She still calls me 'that Smith brat.' "

He drew a deep breath. "Right now we'd better check on the—no, we've already done that. Let's do the square. This side first. Be sure you ask everyone about the cat. And ask them to check their cellars and back gardens."

While Mr. Smith was dividing the houses along the two sides of the square among Peter, Nancy, and the children, Poppy edged around until she was behind him. As the others headed for the square, she ducked

132

out of sight behind one of the neighbors' tall hydrangea bushes. Only Cisco noticed. He caught a glimpse of her pink-polka-dotted green T-shirt behind the branches and fat blue blooms. He almost followed, but his father's anxious gaze swung around and caught him.

"Oh, sorry, Cisco. I missed you. I'm going to do the middle of the far side of the square. You can start at the Dawson Street end."

Mr. Smith hurried up Hillyard Street. Cisco followed reluctantly. Boo fell into step beside him.

"Did you find that old newspaper article?" she asked.

In all the bustle of tree climbing and Babba's disappearance, Cisco had forgotten his mission to the library. Alarmed, he clapped a hand on the front pocket of his shorts. The little notebook was still there.

Boo held her hand out. "Let me see."

She skimmed through the scribbled notes. As they reached the corner she came to the swindlers' names. From her own pocket she brought a pencil and folded sheet of paper and copied the names at the foot of her own list.

"Here's your notebook." She thrust it at him and took off at a trot after the others.

Cisco hesitated. His father was already out of sight across the square, but he did not want to follow. He was sure that going from house to house was a waste of time. Poppy had the right idea.

Cisco turned and dashed back down Hillyard Street.

* * *

Poppy did exactly what Babba had done. She began at
the ramshackle porch. Tiptoeing, peering everywhere,
she made her way back toward the front of the house.
In the soft earth beside one junk pile, she saw the print
of one small foot, then nothing more. Carefully, she
tried each of the cellar windows. Each was as grimy
and fast shut as the one before, until she came to the
very last one, opposite the trash cans. That window
was open, just a crack. There was a small, smeary
handprint near the frame on one side and a jumble of
small fingerprints on the other. Poppy dropped to her
hands and knees and gave the window a quick, nervous
push.

"Babba? . . . *Babba?*"

For a moment Poppy heard nothing. Then there
was a rustle of movement, a sniffle, and an odd, soft,
scrabbly rattle.

"Poppy? Poppy, tum det me." Babba's whimper
came between sniffles. "I tan't det out."

"I will if you don't baby-talk," Poppy hissed, and
then was sorry. Babba usually used her baby-talk act
only on strangers. Perhaps she really was frightened.
"Here—reach."

Poppy stretched out flat on the ground and wormed
her way in far enough to hold the window open with her
head. She reached one arm down inside. Her fingertips
met the coal heap. Babba's attacks had spread it further
out across the floor, lowering it by almost a foot.

134

"I can't," Babba insisted.

As Poppy's eyes grew used to the darkness of the cellar room, she saw that Babba really couldn't reach. She was too small and the coal heap too large. Poppy bit her lip.

"I guess I can come down and boost you up," she said doubtfully. It would not be easy. Feetfirst would be safest, but she didn't like the thought of lying back flat to wriggle through. How would she keep the window from banging down on her nose or chin? Her insides fluttered nervously.

"*Ssst!* Not that way, silly!"

"Cisco!" Poppy's butterflies vanished. "Babba's down in the coal cellar," she whispered. "She can't climb up."

Cisco took a moment to wedge the low window open with a short length of wood.

"Okay, but go in facedown so you can hang on to the windowsill. And if you slide, you can use your hands and feet to slow yourself down. Here—scrooch yourself in, and I'll hang on."

In a moment Poppy was scrambling to her feet at the foot of the coal pile. "Are you okay?" she whispered to Babba. "Give me your hand. I'll boost you up to Cisco."

It didn't work. Poppy was three years older, but not much bigger than her little sister. With Babba's weight pushing down at her, she sank ankle-deep and then floundered knee-deep in the coal. Each struggling step she took brought them only an inch or two higher.

"Hang on," Cisco whispered. "I'll find something for Babba to hold on to."

Soon he was back with an old broom. The bristles were worn down to a stump. Cisco stuck the stumpy end down through the window.

"Grab on, Babba," he whispered. "Poppy'll push and I'll pull."

It was hard work and slow. Inch by inch Babba struggled up toward the window. Cisco was panting and Poppy breathless.

"Hold on," Cisco wheezed.

Me-owr.

"Cookie!" Babba let go of the broom. "We forgot Cookie!" She wriggled around and churned her way back down the coal heap.

Poppy made a grab, but Babba zigged then zagged to snatch up the basket she had dropped when Poppy appeared.

Poppy darted after her into the furnace room. "We don't have *time*," she hissed. "Everybody is looking all over for you. Daddy's going to call the police. Come *on*."

"In a minute," Babba said. "I have to bring the kitties so Cookie will come."

"That's stealing," Poppy protested. "They belong here."

"Do not." Babba knelt in front of the furnace and

reached in through the ash door. Cookie watched anxiously as she brought out one kitten, dropped it into the basket, and reached in for another.

"I bet Mrs. Witch doesn't even know she's got kittens. She only likes big, fat cats."

Poppy blinked. "Fat cats?"

Babba tucked a third kitten into the basket. "She's got lots. In Rumpelstiltskin's room."

Poppy frowned, but just as she was about to say, "Don't be silly," a sharp voice sliced through the darkness.

"Not there, my pet. In the cupboard. Hurry. Hurry!"

Poppy jumped and almost squeaked aloud in fright. The voice had come from somewhere close by, but there was no one in the room. "There's no such things as witches," she whispered to herself with a shiver. "There's *not*."

Babba pointed at the old vent grate at the foot of the wall, then turned back to tuck a fourth kitten into the basket. Poppy knelt and bent over to peer into the room beyond. Her eyes widened.

"Oh, gosh," she breathed, so softly that she scarcely heard herself. Then she rose and, stepping quietly, made for the coal-cellar door.

Cisco was still crouched by the window.

"Where's Babba?" he demanded. "We've got to hurry. For gosh sakes, if the cops come and the Wicked Witch finds you down there, you'll get arrested."

"No." Poppy, her face a pale blur in the cellar's darkness, shook her head violently. "You come down. Quick. You've got to see. You've *got* to."

The room on the other side of the furnace-room wall was the strangest Cisco had ever seen.

But that wasn't the half of it.

17

BOO SAT ON GRANDMA SMITH'S FRONT PORCH, WAITING FOR the others to come back from the square. While she waited, she unfolded the sheets of paper on which she had listed the swindlers' names and descriptions. If only she could figure out what it was about the ten names that niggled at her! She stared hard at the list—as if she could hypnotize herself into lifting letters off the page and making them spell out the answer. The letters began to squirm, like letters written with teeny-tiny ants instead of pencil, but all that did was make her head ache. She stopped when she began to see double and quadruple.

Except—did people ever *see* quadruple?

Not, she decided, unless every name in the list had double letters already. And they actually, oddly, did. She began to underline them: Wo*ll*er, U*ll*man, Penny-man, Ni*ss*ler, La*rr*imore, Ba*kk*us, De*nn*ison, Fo*ss*ick, Ha*ll*inan, Je*ff*ries. Boo scowled. It could be a weird coincidence, but . . .

Perhaps it would help if she rearranged the names

into a diagram, like—like what? Like the pattern of the stolen houses on a map? That probably wouldn't prove a thing.

Then by dates? That was easy enough.

The five cases from Cisco's notes about the old newspaper article had appeared—according to Cisco's scribbled note, *"In order"*—listed by date already. She copied them down again on the back of the first sheet. Then she added the five from Cisco's "legwork" list, rearranged in order of the house thefts.

Nothing. Nothing at all.

Absentmindedly Boo began to doodle with the capital letters of the names, darkening them as her pencil wandered down the list. *A, B. C, D. E—F—G* . . . She stared, and then began to scribble faster.

> **A**lbert **B**akkus
> **C**harles **D**ennison
> **E**ugene **F**ossick
> **G**eorge **H**allinan
> **I**an **J**effries
> **K**enneth **L**arrimore
> **M**arvin **N**issler
> **O**scar **P**ennyman
> **S**idney **T**. **U**llman
> **V**ictor **W**oller

S, T, U, V, W—

"Somebody's got to be playing games!" Boo exclaimed.

Grandma, who was sitting in her wheelchair at the end of the porch, broke off talking to Mrs. Finnerty across their porch railings.

"What's that, Boo dear?" With a quick look to check on Danny, asleep on the porch swing, she wheeled around to face Boo.

Boo scrambled to her feet.

"Look here, Grandma. These are all the swindlers in order of the houses that got stolen, and lookit! They're made-up names. They've got to be. See—all the last names have double letters in them. That could be a coincidence, I guess, but the capital letters couldn't. They go from *A-B-C* right through the alphabet, Except for *Q* and *R*."

"And *X, Y,* and *Z.* So they do," Grandma said. She sounded a bit doubtful. "But what can it mean?"

Nancy and Peter, back from searching their share of the square, joined them.

"Let's see," said Nancy. "Holy Hannibal, that is funny. Maybe the chief crook is one of those weirdos who leave clues so they'll be caught."

"The missing *Q* and *R* could mean there's another stolen house," Peter suggested. "One Cisco and Lee didn't turn up. And Nancy's right—the double letters and the alphabet could be ways to try to catch somebody's attention. Sort of like saying 'Yah, yah, yah!'— a way to thumb their noses at anybody who caught on after they got away."

A moment later Mr. Smith came hurrying down from the square. "I'm calling the cops," he announced grimly as he strode indoors. The screen door slammed behind him.

Boo looked around for Poppy, but she was nowhere to be seen. Cisco was gone, too. She frowned down at the lists, then folded them and stuck them back into her pocket. The grown-ups were busy talking all at once. No one noticed as she stood up, stretched, and wandered out to the sidewalk and down Hillyard Street.

"*Pss-st!*" came the hiss from Mrs. Tuttlebee's cellar window.

Boo, startled, almost crashed backward into the garbage cans. "Cisco?" She crouched down beside the window and peered in. After a moment she could make out three pale, smudged faces below, and the cat-gleam of Cookie's eyes.

"You kids are crazy," she hissed. "What are you all doing down there? Babba—are you okay?"

Babba nodded her dusty gray curls happily. She held up the basket. "I got kittens. *Five*," she whispered.

"Oh boy, won't Grandma be tickled?" Boo said sourly. "I guess you'd better hand them up, Cisco, and then give Babba a boost. We have to get home fast. Daddy's calling the police."

Three heads shook an urgent *no!*

"I think," said Cisco, "you'd better come see, and quick."

18

THE ROOM BOO SAW THROUGH THE OLD VENT'S GRATE WAS amazing. The heavy curtains drawn back at each end of the French windows were a dark cherry red with gold tassels and bobbles along their tops and edges. The sofas and armchairs, footstools and other chairs all were covered in cherry- or rose- or strawberry-colored velvet, and most had bobbles around their skirts. The lamp shades were a yellowy ivory color, and even they had the bobbles around their bottoms. The carpet was all roses, rose-colored, pink, and ivory.

"Yuck!" Boo whispered in Poppy's ear. "It looks like a picture off a really weird valentine."

The children could not see the far-right end of the room, but on the near end to the left, tall cupboards flanked a marble-fronted fireplace. A silver candelabra stood at each end of the wide, carved marble mantelpiece. A large gold-framed mirror hung above it.

But the room—and the cats—weren't the half of it.

On one of the hottest days of the year, a large fire blazed in the fancy fireplace. Back and forth between the fire and the cornermost cupboard darted old Mrs. Tuttlebee. A small, balding man in shorts—Babba's Rumpelstiltskin!—followed at her heels, flapping his hands in distress as Mrs. Tuttlebee threw one sheaf of papers after another onto the fire.

"No, no! Not that way. They only burn around the edges if you throw 'em in in wads. Just do a couple of sheets at a time and crumple 'em up, like I did in the bonfire the other day. Every scrap's got to burn."

The old lady's black eyes snapped. She thrust the papers at him. "You do it, then, and be quick about it. If that little Smith brat hasn't been found yet, her blockhead of a father's called the police by now. We have to get rid of everything you can't take with you. I'll fetch your makeup stuff and hairpieces."

The little man dropped the papers and made a dash around the old lady to put himself between her and the doors to the cupboard nearest the fireplace.

"Oh, no you don't! Some of those rugs cost hundreds. And I'll need all that stuff out in Saint Louis."

Poppy backed away from the grate, where she and Boo had crouched together. She breathed a soft question into Cisco's ear. "Why does she want to burn his rugs?"

Cisco was mystified, too. He shrugged and put a finger to his lips, then knelt to take Poppy's place at the grate.

The little man in the overdressed room flung both

cupboard doors open wide, revealing on the top two shelves rows of head-shaped Styrofoam blocks. Each was topped with a wig or toupee. Cisco's eyes widened. Disguises! Then—of course! Poppy's trash-can mustache had been Rumpelstiltskin's, too.

"Don't you dare burn 'em," the little man warned shrilly. "I just forgot to pack 'em." Climbing onto a chair, he snatched one hairpiece after another from the plastic blocks and rolled them into a hairy wad. He jammed them into a large leather suitcase that lay open on the table nearest the cupboard. From the bottom shelves he scooped up several pairs of shoes— odd, clunky shoes with high, built-up soles, and crammed those in, too. Old Mrs. Tuttlebee darted in and pulled from the shelves as many plastic wig blocks as she could carry.

"Just how do you figure you're going to get away even if you do get all your gear packed up?" she wheezed. "The car's out front where the whole street can see it, not down below. If the police see any of this stuff, they'll put two and two together faster'n you can sneeze."

She pushed him out of the way. "Serves you right for sticking around so long this time. You'll be singing a different tune from your 'They'll never know, never guess.' "

"Ma! Don't burn those wig blocks!" the little man yelled. "The plastic fumes'll stink the place up, and likely smother us in the bargain."

Poppy was frantic to see what was going on. She

145

tugged at Cisco's shirt until he finally stood and stepped back. Boo stood, too, and made pointing gestures toward the coal cellar. Cisco and Poppy would rather have stayed to watch, but they followed. Babba and the basket, followed by an anxious Cookie, brought up the rear.

"What is it? What's going on in there?" Cisco demanded as Boo eased the door shut behind them.

Boo's eyes shone in the dim light.

"He's him. *Him.* The swindler!"

Poppy blinked. "Who? The one who's trying to steal our house?"

"Not just him. *All* of them. Look—" Boo pulled from her pocket the lists of names and handed the according-to-dates list to Cisco. "Don't you see? He made all those names up. And then he made the people up—and made himself up as all of them. That's what the wigs and makeup stuff are for. The elevator shoes are to make him ordinary-short instead of short-short. And I bet it's the fake deeds and stuff they're burning."

Poppy jiggled up and down with excitement. "But, Boo! Didn't you hear? He called the Wicked Witch 'Ma.' He's Stanley! The 'shrimpy little boy.' That's what he thought nobody would ever, ever guess. His name!"

"Like Rumpelstiltskin," said Babba with an I-told-you-so nod.

Boo stared. Cisco blinked. Stanley Tuttlebee! The

boy who ran away. It could all fit—*did* all fit—even the long-ago part when Rufus the roofer was Mrs. Tuttlebee's roomer.

Boo wished she had figured it out herself. Cisco was sure in another minute he would have.

"What are we waiting for, then?" he whispered. "We have to go tell the police. If Daddy called them, they might even be here already."

"They won't believe us," Poppy said anxiously. "They'll think we made it all up."

Boo considered. "Maybe. But Daddy'll believe us, and I bet the police'll believe *him*. Only, they'll have to get a search warrant, and by then all the proof'll be burned up."

Cisco caught his breath. "No, it won't. Not if"—his eyes glowed in his smudgy face—"not if they have a good reason to think the Wicked Witch is holding us prisoner. Then they'd have a 'reasonable cause' to come right in." At least, that was the way it worked on TV detective shows.

Boo nodded. Cisco always was good at plots. "Okay, but how?" she asked. "Throw a note out the window and just hope Nancy finds it?"

"We could send Babba," Poppy ventured.

It was settled. Boo would write the note. Then she and Cisco and Poppy would make a human ladder for Babba to climb up. Babba would carry the note in her kitten basket and *run*. She was to find Grandma if she didn't see their father right away.

Boo was pleased with the note. *"HELP PLEASE HELP,"* it read. *"Mrs. Tuttlebee has us trapped in her coal cellar."*

"It's not exactly a fib. We *are* sort of trapped. And they'll have to come through the fancy weird room to find us and let us out."

The human ladder was not so easy. Keeping as quiet as possible was important, so they couldn't shovel the coal aside and have Cisco stand on Boo's shoulders while they gave Babba a hand up and Poppy boosted. At first they tried sitting back against the coal heap one above the other, knees bent, feet on the shoulders below. They ended up scrunched together at the bottom.

The plan that finally worked was the most uncomfortable of all. Boo had to clear and dust off a patch of floor at the base of the heap so that her feet wouldn't slip, lie back flat on the slope of hard, knobbly coal, and let Cisco clamber up over her so that he could turn, plant his feet on her shoulders, and lie back flat himself. Poppy, at least, was lighter. Even so, making the ladder took a lot of muffled *oof*ing and *ouch*ing and clattering down of coal.

"Everybody be *quiet*," Boo gasped as she reached out to take Babba's hand. "And for gosh sakes, walk where there's bones, not soft spots."

Babba, being Babba, was careful and quick. A minute later she was pushing the basket of kittens through the window. Climbing through it herself was harder because all of the wallowing and clambering had lowered the coal pile. But then, with a boost from Poppy, she was up and gone. Boo, sore and breathless, sat up. Cisco, and then Poppy, slid down the coal to pile up against her.

"I just got it," Boo gasped. "I bet 'Mr. Zimmerman's' initials are supposed to be X. Y. He *was* saying 'Yah, yah, yah!' to everybody. *He's* X. Y. Z."

For a moment no one said a word. Then Poppy whispered timidly, "But the note really was a fib, Boo."

"Oh, for—" Boo began. She was stopped by Cisco's sharp nudge.

"No," he croaked, "it's not a fib."

His sisters followed his stare to the furnace-room door as it swung slowly open. They blinked.

Rumpelstiltskin and the Wicked Witch stood in the doorway, blinking back at them.

19

MR. SMITH HANDED BABBA'S NOTE TO OLD MR. HAVLICHEK
and ran a hand through his hair so that it stood up
even more wildly than before. "I don't understand,"
he said helplessly. "Why would Mrs. Tuttlebee *want*
to shut my kids up in her coal cellar?"

"To give them a scare because they were snooping?"
Peter suggested.

"Then why shouldn't I just go in there and haul
them out?"

"Because," Gus Havlichek explained, "if the old
girl's really gone off her rocker, you don't want to
push her. When the police get here, they can work out
what's safest. You don't want to take a chance on the
kids getting hurt."

"You're right. Of course not." Mr. Smith drew a
deep breath. He looked down at the small coal-black-
ened figure whose arms were wrapped around his leg.

"Babba, are you *sure* Boo didn't tell you to tell us
anything more?"

Babba shook her head. "Uh-uh." She gave him her

best blue-eyed baby-doll look. "Please, Daddy, can I go take a baff now?"

"Can you—oh. Yes, I suppose so." Mr. Smith looked around almost as if he expected to see a bathtub in the street. His mind was on Poppy and Cisco and Boo.

"I'll take her on up to her grandma," Mrs. Finnerty offered.

"And I'll look after Cookie's kittens," Gus Havlichek promised. He scooped up the basket. "Just until you can talk to your granny about 'em, Missy Barbara."

When Babba was gone, Mr. Smith looked anxiously up toward Oakland Square as he dusted off the leg of his jeans. "Where are the cops? They said they'd be right here."

Peter looked at his watch as Mr. Havlichek headed home with the basket of kittens. "They'll be here. They said fifteen minutes. It's only been—fourteen."

Ten minutes later Mr. Smith, Peter, and Nancy were standing in the same anxious knot outside Mrs. Tuttlebee's gate. The police still had not arrived. A second phone call and the news of Babba's note had brought the report that Lieutenant Delatorre had radioed in that he was on his way out from downtown. A second squad car would follow in minutes. The first had been delayed helping out at a three-car crash on the parkway.

At five minutes past seven, Mrs. Tuttlebee's roomer, Mr. Zimmerman, opened Mrs. Tuttlebee's front door.

He smoothed his sleek black hair and straightened his tie primly. Picking up his sample cases, he stepped onto the porch, put down one case, then closed the door and the screen door, picked up the case, and made his way out the front walk.

Mr. Smith and the others met him at the front gate.

"Mr.—er, Zimmerman?" asked Mr. Smith.

Mr. Zimmerman blinked. "That's me," he said timidly.

"Have you seen any kids in or around your house this evening?" Mr. Smith asked anxiously. "Two girls, eight and twelve, and a boy, ten."

"No." Mr. Zimmerman seemed bewildered. He set down his cases on the sidewalk. "I've never seen children here." He cleared his throat. "I believe Mrs. Tuttlebee is not a person who would care to have children around."

"Well, have you seen Mrs. Tuttlebee?"

"No, but she is in. I heard her television shouting away downstairs." He sniffed prissily. "*And* I smelled onions frying. Dreadful odor! I microwave my own little meals upstairs," he explained shyly.

"You've been in all evening?"

"Since five forty-five," said Mr. Zimmerman.

Peter eyed the sample cases. "It's a little late to be going to work, isn't it?"

Mr. Zimmerman gave his watch an anxious glance. "I have an eight o'clock appointment with the buyer at Allen's in Monroeville. They're open late on Wednesdays."

"Sorry to keep you," Mr. Smith said quickly. "Just one more question. Is there any way into the house besides the side porch and front and back doors?"

Mr. Zimmerman shook his head. "I don't know. I see only the front door, the front stairs, and my own two rooms on the second floor." With a polite nod he made his way to his car.

Lieutenant Delatorre's car turned down Hillyard Street just as the shiny black Buick vanished from sight along Oakland Square. The patrol car appeared moments later.

Lieutenant Delatorre frowned when he was shown Babba's note.

"And Zimmerman said he heard Mrs. Tuttlebee's TV turned on loud," Mr. Smith reported. " 'Shouting,' I think he said. But maybe it wasn't the TV. It could have been her."

"We'll find out, Dan. You'd better wait out here."

He signaled to one of the two officers to check the back of the house, and then, with the other, headed up the porch steps. Mr. Smith and the two young people were watching anxiously when Danny's voice piped up behind them.

"I'm glad that other man's gone. He's *mean*," Danny announced. "S'afternoon he said I touched his ol' car. But I din't."

"Danny, what in blazes are you doing down here? I told you to stay with Grandma."

"Grandma took Babba into her baffroom to make her take a baff. She told me to wait right outside."

"She meant outside the bathroom, you imp."

"I am outside the baffroom."

Peter choked back a hoot of laughter. "It's okay. We'll hold on to him."

Lieutenant Delatorre knocked loudly at the front door. After a moment he knocked again. Still no answer.

"The old lady's not deaf, is she?"

Mr. Smith shook his head. "I don't know."

Lieutenant Delatorre tried the doorknob, and the door opened. He turned to look back at the others with a solemn wink. "Could be deaf, could be dead. I guess we'll just have to play it safe and go in to take a look around, won't we? We'll start in the coal cellar and work our way up. You folks stay put, okay?"

Mr. Smith was no better than Danny at staying put. Two fidgety minutes went by, and then he strode into the Tuttlebee house. Nancy and Peter followed cautiously, with Danny.

They stopped in the gloomy front hall to stare.

Peter shuddered. "Talk about grim, ghastly grunge!"

The air had a stale, musty odor, and the floor was dark with a good twenty or thirty years' worth of dust and grime. Everywhere they looked there were newspapers. Newspapers and magazines. Tied up in neat

154

bundles, they were stacked like huge bricks up the walls, blocking the front windows. The side window on the right was clear, but there were stacks alongside the front staircase and even up the first flight of steps. Only a narrow path had been left open to allow passage to the second floor. To the left of the front hall, the sliding panels of a wide doorway stood halfway open. Except for a narrow pathway across to a window, the room beyond was crammed with dusty furniture and junk. Near the door a broken hat stand, a wicker baby buggy without wheels, and a rusty set of bedsprings were piled on top of a mouse-eaten sofa.

Beyond the junk room, stacked bundles of newspapers lined a hallway that led back into the depths of the house. The passage was more like a tunnel than a hall. About two-and-a-half feet wide, it was so low that the men, and Nancy, had to hunch over to enter. It led between stacks of neat bundles of papers. About halfway to the ceiling, boards had been laid across the passage like a roof. Then more newspaper bundles had been added to fill in solid the upper part of the original hallway.

"Good gravy!" Nancy gasped. "I've been living on top of *this*? It must be the world's worst firetrap."

Peter shook his head in wonder. "The old bat must be loony as a bedbug."

Mr. Smith looked more worried than ever.

From somewhere up ahead came the slam of a screen

door. Apparently the third police officer had found his way in at the back of the house.

One of the police officers called softly, "Yo! I think I've found the cellar door. Take a right turn at the kitchen. Then it's the first door on the right."

He paused. "Hold on a minute—there's got to be a light switch somewhere. Hah!—got it."

The three police officers were already out of sight when Mr. Smith and the others reached the cellar stairs. From below came two loud knocks. The lieutenant's voice called, "Police! Open up, Mrs. Tuttlebee." After a silence, there were loud thumping noises and the sound of splintering wood.

Mr. Smith wavered at the top of the stairs for a moment, but then started down.

The foot of the linoleum-covered steps faced a blank wall. On the right a bare, narrow hallway doubled back past the stairwell. Halfway along on the left hand a door stood ajar. At the end, a heavier door with two large brass locks stood wide open, its door frame splintered.

The long room beyond with its window wall, its cats, and its fancy candy-box finery was such a surprise after the dirt and clutter upstairs that everyone except Danny stood and gaped.

Danny pulled free of Nancy's hand and dashed to the center of the cushiony, cherry-colored room. He squatted down to pick up a coin from the center of a carpet rose.

"Looky! It's a dime. I found a dime, Daddy!"

"Danny, you'd find a penny on a pitch-dark prairie," said Mr. Smith. He looked around the room anxiously.

Lieutenant Delatorre appeared behind them in the other doorway that opened off the hall. "You should have stayed outside, Dan."

"I couldn't. Besides, the more of us there are to search this place, the better. It's a maze." Mr. Smith tried to see past the lieutenant into the dimly lit room beyond.

"What's in there?"

"Furnace room and coal cellar. But your kids aren't here."

One of the uniformed officers joined them. She held out a tight, coal-grimed wad of paper. "I just found this, though, sir."

Lieutenant Delatorre, using the cap end of his pen, teased it open. Holding the two sheets together by one corner, he unfolded it gingerly.

"That's Boo's writing," Mr. Smith exclaimed as he peered at the topmost sheet. "There's where she tore a strip off for the note."

"Now, I wonder why she threw this away?" The lieutenant frowned at the lists of names. "It reminds me, though: I took a look at those grant deeds. The same Greensburg notary witnessed all five, but it turns out she died late last year. All five seals and signatures are forgeries."

Mr. Smith only nodded. He was too worried about the children to care.

"Right, let's get moving," Lieutenant Delatorre said. "Collins, you'd better radio for some backup. We have to search that rabbit warren upstairs. Bachman and I'll get a start on it right now."

Mr. Smith, Nancy, Danny, and Peter stayed behind in the rose-and-cherry-colored room and hunted everywhere for some other trace of the children. They looked under sofas and chairs, behind curtains, and in cupboards, and searched two bedrooms that opened off the rear end of the room. Peter even knocked at the backs of cupboards and peered under carpets.

"For secret doors or a trapdoor," he explained. "In a place like this, who knows?"

They found an unlocked, empty safe behind a framed picture, but no sign of the missing children. Nancy, giving up, headed for the stairway to join the search on the floors above.

"Peter, I think you'd better take Danny home," Mr. Smith called back over his shoulder as he followed.

"Sure thing," Peter said.

But Danny pulled back as Peter caught him by the arm. "No, looky!" he crowed. "I founded another one."

He pointed to a small silver spot on the carpet under an end table.

"Yeah, great," Peter said impatiently. "Okay, get it, *then* we go home."

Danny had other ideas. Where there were two dimes, there could be three. Or four. He picked up the dime and then made a dash for the French windows and the spot where he had found the first coin.

Peter was just as fast. "Gotcha!" he cried. He scooped Danny up and slung him under his arm. Danny was a chunky, solid little boy, a lot heavier than Peter had expected. And stronger.

"No!" Danny kicked. "There's 'nother one. Lemme go!"

And there was another one. Just outside the French door at the end of the row of windows, at the edge of a stone path, a third dime glimmered. An inch further and it would have been hidden by the neat hedge that bordered the walkway along the side of the house.

Peter set Danny down and tried the door. It was unlocked and opened at a touch. Danny shot out to scoop up the third dime.

Peter began to be curious. "Can I see, Danny?"

Danny opened a chubby fist to show the three coins.

"Hey, lucky you!" said Peter. "Better hold on to 'em tight."

All three were old genuine silver coins, not the sandwich kind with silver on both sides and copper in the middle. They could be valuable. Peter frowned. It looked almost as if they had dropped through a hole in someone's pocket. Or in a money bag, for that matter. A bag from an empty safe . . . ?

"I see '*nother* one!" Danny stood at a break in the hedge. At his feet a flight of steep stone steps led to a narrow path down through the trees. He pointed to the path.

Peter grabbed him away just in time.

The dime was there.

So, twenty-five or thirty yards further down, was a straggly row of suitcases and a small mound of bulging carrier bags. The Wicked Witch was sitting on an up-ended suitcase. From further on down the path, Mr. Zimmerman came puffing uphill toward her.

20

LIEUTENANT DELATORRE HELD HIS RADIO TO HIS EAR. "SAY that again!"

"*. . . both on the hill . . . cars on the way down to Boundary Road . . . Code 2.*" The sound reception inside the house was uneven.

"Good. Better get another team over here to work down from the top. I can't spare anyone up here until we find the kids."

Mr. Smith edged past him to explore toward the end of the low, narrow hallway that led to the side porch. "Boo! Poppy! Cisco! Where are you?" he shouted. "Boo? *Boo!*"

"Mr. Smith—" Nancy, a little way ahead, held up a hand. "I thought I heard something."

Mr. Smith stopped to listen. There *was* a voice calling, but the sound was muffled and seemed to come from somewhere above.

"*Addy! Uhsdairs!*"

In a moment Mr. Smith was hurrying back toward

the front hall and stairs. Nancy and the police were close behind.

The newspapers petered out halfway to the second floor. Upstairs was all junk. Much of it was small junk that looked as if it had come from Mrs. Tuttlebee's years of scavenging in neighborhood trash cans. Every room was a giant trash can.

"Boo! Cisco! Keep calling!"

"*Addy! Ere! Uhsdairs!*"

"Lieutenant! This way!" one police officer called.

As the lieutenant and Mr. Smith turned the corner into the back hallway, the cries grew louder and clearer. "Daddy! Here! The stairs. On the stairs!"

The officer pointed to the end of the hall, where an old mattress and a tangle of rusty pipe and ragged window screen had been propped up to hide a door.

"I'm here, kids," Mr. Smith called. "Are you all okay?"

"We're fine," said Boo.

"Only it's dark in here," Poppy added anxiously.

"Hang on. We'll have you out in a minute, sweetie."

It took two minutes. The rubbish and mattress were cleared away in no time, but the locked door took longer. It was a heavy door, made of oak, and could not be knocked down without endangering the children trapped on the stairway behind it.

"Kick in one of the bottom panels," Lieutenant Delatorre ordered. "You kids, get as far down as you can and turn your backs."

"We can't go down," Cisco objected. "The steps are full of junk."

"Then move over as far as you can away from the side where the door handle is."

It took five kicks of the officer's heavy shoe. Once the splintered shards of the panel were pulled out, Poppy crawled through first, then Cisco. For Boo it was a tighter squeeze. Mr. Smith gave her a hand.

"Daddy," Boo panted. "It was him all the time. Every time he came home to Pittsburgh. He was Rufus the roofer and the storm-window man and all the house stealers."

" 'Him' who, honey?"

"Yes, 'him' who?" the lieutenant echoed.

"Her son! Mrs. Tuttlebee's son," Cisco and Poppy said together.

Mr. Smith and Lieutenant Delatorre stared at each other in disbelief. "*Stanley Tuttlebee?* Sneaky Stan?"

"Holy mackerel!" the lieutenant marveled.

Mr. Smith grinned. "I guess we shouldn't be so surprised. When we were in first grade and he was in fifth, he used to steal our lunch money, remember?"

"I do. Look," the lieutenant said, "you all better come with me." He led the way back down the hall.

"I'll go tell Mrs. Smith and Mrs. Finnerty the kids are okay," Nancy said.

"But there's more," Boo said breathlessly as she brought up the rear. "When they locked us up, we

163

heard Mrs. Tuttlebee say, 'You go fix up as Zimmerman again, and I'll see to the money.' "

"Zimmerman is *Stan?*" Mr. Smith looked dazed, and then dismayed.

"So we didn't save Grandma's house after all," Cisco said. "'Cause they burned up all the evidence, and—"

"And they g-got a-w-w-way," Poppy gulped as she hurried at her father's heels.

"They haven't yet," Lieutenant Delatorre said. "I got a radio call just before we heard you kids shouting. It seems your little brother may have caught them for us."

"*Danny?*" Cisco stumbled down the last step before the front-stair landing.

"That's right. He and young Quilty spotted their escape route." The lieutenant held the front door open. "We'll go in my car. We may be in time to catch the end of the show."

Boundary Street, along the bottom of the hill, had no houses, only a high retaining wall on one side, and on the other a fence and the railway tracks beyond. The police car blocking Boundary Street moved to let the lieutenant's blue sedan pass. Two more police cars were drawn up alongside the wall, one on each side of the lane opening, but some yards clear of it. Both were safely out of sight of the car parked in the short, steep lane.

Lieutenant Delatorre drove slowly past. The big

164

black car sat in the lane, apparently empty. Cisco leaned excitedly over the front seat.

"That's the same place where Lee and I saw the car this afternoon! I bet all the time he just pretended to go off every day—and then parked here and walked up the back way home again."

"Could be."

The lieutenant drove on a little further, then turned around in the middle of the street and pulled up behind the parked police car. The two people watching from its backseat turned to wave, and the Smiths recognized Peter Quilty and Lee Chiang. Peter must have delivered Danny to Grandma and then joined the search party. Lee apparently had heard about the search for Babba and come to Hillyard Street in time for the excitement. He knew where the path came out and must have shown the police the black car's parking place.

One of the officers from the car ahead walked back to lean down at the lieutenant's window.

"Sir, the suspect stowed a load of stuff in the trunk of the car and went back up the path. From what the older kid says, there's an old lady and another fair-sized load to come down."

Lieutenant Delatorre turned to Mr. Smith. "This whole operation is so neat and twisty that I'll bet you fifty bucks Sneaky Stan's had a lot of practice. I'd say he's been pretty busy in the big, wide world when he's been away from Pittsburgh."

The officer's radio crackled. *"Here they come."*

The lieutenant pulled the blue sedan out from behind the squad car. "We'll play at being passing traffic. Keep down low enough so they won't recognize you."

The Smiths, hunched down, were all eyes.

At the top of the little lane, where the path met the steep pavement, they saw "Mr. Zimmerman." He was laden down with a cardboard box clamped under one arm, two suitcases, and a briefcase. Mrs. Tuttlebee came several yards behind, teetering down the path, carrying a bulging canvas carryall in each hand.

Then the lieutenant's car was past and pulling up beside the wall. Moments later the two squad cars moved to block the entrance to the lane. The Smiths tumbled out of the car to follow Lieutenant Delatorre.

Mrs. Tuttlebee was seated in the black car. Stanley Tuttlebee stood frozen by the driver's door. Then he turned toward the upward path, but saw two more police officers coming down from above.

Lieutenant Delatorre stopped in the middle of the lane, hands in his pockets, and grinned. Mr. Smith came to stand beside him.

"Hi, Stan," he said. "Stolen any lunch money lately?"

21

Friday, July 30,
and six weeks later

THE SMITHS ARRIVED HOME FROM COURT FRIDAY AFTER-
noon and telephoned Mrs. Smith at their old neighbors', the Maldonados', in Los Angeles. It was her first
day out of the hospital.

"Momma!" Boo snatched her chance to get in the
first word when her mother answered. She almost
shouted into the phone. "We saved all the houses. We
really did! Here's Daddy."

"Hi, hon." Mr. Smith cradled the receiver between
his shoulder and his ear as he fended off the other
children's reaching hands. "How've you been feeling?
Uh-huh. Yeah, I know. It's grisly having to stay in bed
all day, but you know what the doc said. It's only a
few more weeks. What? Oh, we just got back from the
special court hearing. The judge postponed our case—
Mr. Fazio's, too—until the police investigation's finished. Look, all the kids are itching to talk to you.
Here's Boo again."

"Momma—" Boo began. "What? Oh, no, it didn't

get all burned up after all. There were some copies he got made of the real deeds that just got frizzled around the edges. They're how he knew just how to make out the fake deeds. He—" She broke off. "Cut it *out*, Cisco. Momma? Cisco wants to talk, too."

Cisco grabbed the receiver to hear his mother say, "Hi, Cisco honey. What's this that Grandma was telling me Wednesday night about *Danny* catching the crooks?"

"Crumbs, Momma, he didn't catch anybody," Cisco said. "He just helped find where they disappeared to, but only by accident. And guess what? The cops took pictures of Sneaky Stan in all his disguises and sent them out by some special machine over the phone— yeah, fax—to all the other police forces. Lots of them phoned back to say he stole houses there, too."

Cisco talked even faster as Babba gave the phone cord an impatient tug. "And guess what else? After the cops broke the door to Mrs. Tuttlebee's back stairs to let us out, they found all the junk piled in there was stuff she stole from people she got mad at. Daddy's old junior-high wrestling trophy was in there, and he won in the peewee weight!"

"Give *me* the phone," Babba demanded. "*I* want to talk to Momma." It might be important to Cisco that small boys sometimes grow up to be tall men, but Babba was interested in more serious matters.

"An' there was a necklace that was Grandma's, with pretty pink beads," said Babba. "An' Grandma said when I'm big as Boo, I can have it."

Poppy, who spoke next, clutched the telephone close. "Oh, Momma, I miss you. I wish you were here day before yesterday. It was like being in a TV show. We rode in the detective's car and saw all the cops hiding while Mr. Zim—I mean Mr. Tuttlebee—was loading stuff in his car."

All Danny had to say when it was his turn was, "I found three dimes, Momma, so now I got eighty-six whole cents and I love you lots."

On the afternoon of the second Friday in September, Mr. Smith and the children drove to the Pittsburgh airport to meet Mrs. Smith and their new baby, Angela Maria Smith. (The Maria was for Mrs. Maldonado.) Even Elvira was dressed in her best for the occasion. She was freshly painted in a handsome midnight blue with a shiny new silver moon, red-and-gold planets, a sprinkling of stars, and a bright new rainbow on her rear end. In the middle-most of the six sturdy seats Mr. Smith had installed in the rear of the van, Angela Maria rode strapped into her new baby car seat. Her admiring brothers and sisters strained as close to watch and touch her as their safety belts allowed.

By the time Elvira had crossed the Fort Pitt Bridge into the city, Mrs. Smith had heard the entire tale of the great Smith house hustle all over again, with sound effects and gestures.

"What *I* want to know," she said, "is what happened in the end about Babba's kittens and Mrs. Tuttlebee's cats."

Babba hardly looked up from the tiny fingers that clutched one of hers. "We had to give 'em all away," she said.

But when the van drew up in front of the house on Hillyard Street, Mrs. Smith saw that Babba had had the last word after all. Grandma sat on the front-porch swing, waving a welcome.

With Cookie in her lap.

ELEMENTARY SCHOOL LIBRARY